Thomas Dunn English

# The Book of rubies

A collection of the most notable love-poems in the English language

Thomas Dunn English

**The Book of rubies**
*A collection of the most notable love-poems in the English language*

ISBN/EAN: 9783337224417

Printed in Europe, USA, Canada, Australia, Japan

Cover: Foto ©Andreas Hilbeck / pixelio.de

More available books at **www.hansebooks.com**

THE

# BOOK OF RUBIES.

# BOOK OF RUBIES:

A COLLECTION OF THE MOST NOTABLE

## Love=Poems

IN THE

## ENGLISH LANGUAGE.

NEW YORK:
CHARLES SCRIBNER & CO.,
124 GRAND STREET.
1866.

TO

THOSE WHO HAVE LOVED,

AND

TO THOSE WHO HAVE BEEN BELOVED,

NO LESS THAN 

TO THOSE WHO LOVE

AND

TO THOSE WHO ARE BELOVED,

THIS COLLECTION OF

𝔏𝔬𝔳𝔢-𝔓𝔬𝔢𝔪𝔰

IS INSCRIBED.

# Introduction.

IT was the intention of the compiler to include, in a volume of moderate size, the most notable of the minor love-poems of the English language, and its dialects, in such order and to such extent as would serve to show the progress of our amatory poetry, while it gave a fair idea of the different style of our poets, and their relative merits in a single field of action. In this, being an endeavor to combine distinct objects in one, there were some difficulties to be encountered; but these did not prove to be insurmountable. It is possible that some may think a few poems admitted into the collection are not the very best specimens of their kind; while others may complain that some poems deserving a place have been omitted. The former censure may be palliated by a declaration, that all that is mainly a matter of taste; and to the latter it may be replied, that some fitting poems may have escaped the compiler's notice. It is believed that the collection will, nevertheless, be found the most complete and best-arranged in its contents, as it is the most elegant in mechanical execution, of any yet issued. Should the volume meet with favour, and arrive at the desired goal of other editions, it is to be hoped that the consequent revision will render it still more perfect of its kind.

Some difficulty was experienced in culling for a work designed for the centre-table, as well as the library, from celebrated writers at different periods. In the Elizabethan age especially, the erotic poets covered some of their finest conceits with the grossest language, rendering the poems unfit for the perusal of persons of delicate minds. At a later period, the puerilities of the pastoral school afforded but little scope for selection. At all times prior to the close of the last century, there was an affectation of classical knowledge which destroyed the fire and fervour of the verse, by pressing the Roman deities most absurdly into the service of the poet. As the compiler had no right to alter or erase, and did not desire to omit passages, his range of selection was considerably decreased. With all this, there was a sufficient mine of wealth to explore—enough, indeed, to make a larger volume —and he availed himself of the treasure at hand as his judgment taught him to do.

The biographical sketches at the close are purposely meagre. To have made them more full was no part of the design. A few salient points of personal history, to gratify the curiosity of the reader, were considered to be sufficient. Where it was thought to be necessary or desirable, in the body of the work, a foot-note has been introduced; but superfluous comment has been scrupulously avoided.

# BOOK OF RUBIES.

## John Skelton.

[Born 1463.   Died 1529.]

MARGARET.

ERRY Margaret
  As midsummer flower,
Gentle as falcon,
  Or hawk of the tower;
With solace and gladness,
Much mirth and no madness,
All good and no badness;
    So joyously,
    So maidenly,
    So womanly
    Her démeaning
    In every thing,
    Far, far pàssing

That I can indite
Or suffice to write
Of merry Margaret
As midsummer flower,
Gentle as falcon,
Or hawk of the tower;
As patient and as still,
And as full of good-will
As fair Isiphil,
Coliander,
Sweet Pomander,
Good Cassander;
Stedfast of thought,
Well made, well wrought
Far may be sought,
Ere you can find
So courteous, so kind,
As merry Margaret
The midsummer flower,
Gentle as falcon,
Or hawk of the tower.

# Sir Thomas Wyat.

[BORN 1503.   DIED 1542.]

A SUPPLICATION.

FORGET not yet the tried intent
Of such a truth as I have meant
My great travail so gladly spent,
     Forget not yet!

Forget not yet when first began
The weary life ye know, since whan
The suit, the service none tell can;
     Forget not yet!

Forget not yet the great essays,
The cruel wrong, the scornful ways,
The painful patience in delays,
     Forget not yet!

Forget not!  O forget not this,
How long ago hath been, and is
The mind that never meant amiss—
     Forget not yet!

Forget not then thine own approved
The which so long hath thee so loved,
Whose steadfast faith yet never moved —
    Forget not this!

---

## THE ONE HE WOULD LOVE.

FACE that should content me wondrous
    well,
    Should not be fat, but lovely to behold,
Of lively look, all grief for to repel
    With right good grace, so would I that it
    should.
Speak without words such words as none can tell,
    Her tress also should be of crispéd gold,
With wit and these perchance I might be tried,
And knit again with knot that should not slide.

## LOVE COMPARED.

FROM these high hills, as when a spring doth
    fall,
  It trilleth down with still and subtle course,
Of this and that, and gathers aye and shall,
  'Till it have just down flowed to stream and
    force,
  Then at the foot it rageth over all:
So fareth love when he hath ta'en a course;
Rage is his rain, resistance 'vaileth none,
The first eschew is remedy alone.

# Henry Howard, Earl of Surrey.

[Born 1516.　Died 1547.]

---

## A Vow.

SET me where as the sun doth parch the
　　green,
　　Or where his beams do not dissolve the
　　　ice,
　In temperate heat, where he is felt and seen,
　　In presence prest of people, mad or wise;

Set me in high, or yet in low degree,
　In longest night, or in the shortest day;
In clearest sky, or where clouds thickest be,
　In lusty youth, or when my hairs are grey:

Set me in heaven, in earth, or else in hell,
　In hill or dale, or in the foaming flood;
Thrall, or at large, alive where so I dwell,
　Sick, or in health, in evil fame, or good,—

Hers I will be, and only with this thought
Content myself, although my chance be naught.

### Give place, ye Lovers.

GIVE place, ye lovers, here before
    That spent your boasts and brags in vain;
My lady's beauty passeth more
    The best of years, I dare well sayen,
Than doth the Sun the candle-light,
Or brightest day the darkest night.

And thereto hath a troth as just,
    As had Penelope the Fair;
For what she saith, ye may it trust,
    As it by writing seal'd were:
And virtues hath she many mo'
Than I with pen have skill to show.

I could rehearse, if that I would,
    The whole offset of Nature's plaint,
When she had lost the perfect mould,
    The like to whom she could not paint:
With wringing hands, how did she cry,
And what she said, I know it aye.

I knew she swore with raging mind,
    Her kingdom only set apart,

There was no loss by law of kind
 That could have gone so near her heart ;
And this was chiefly all her pain :
" She could not make the like again."


Sith Nature thus gave her the praise,
 To be the chiefest work she wrought,
In faith, methink, some better ways
 On your behalf might well be sought,
Than to compare as ye have done,
To match the candle with the Sun.

# Elizabeth Tudor, Queen of England.

[Born 1533. Died 1603.]

----

## ON MY OWN FEELINGS.

GRIEVE, and dare not show my discontent ;
   I love, and yet am forced to seem to hate ;
I do, yet dare not say I ever meant ;
   I seem stark mute, yet inwardly do prate.
I am, and not ; I freeze, and yet am burned,
Since from myself my other self I turned.

My care is like my shadow in the sun,
   Follows me flying, flies when I pursue it ;
Stands and lies by me, does what I have done,
   This too familiar care does make me rue it.
No means I find to rid him from my breast,
Till by the end of things it be suppressed.

Some gentler passions slide into my mind,
   For I am soft and made of melting snow ;
Or be more cruél, Love, and so be kind ;
   Let me or float or sink, be high or low,
Or let me live with some more sweet content,
   Or die, and so forget what love e'er meant.

# John Harrington.

[Born 1534. Died 1582.]

## Sonnet on Isabella Markham.

WHENCE comes my love? O heart, disclose;
It was from cheeks that shamed the rose,
From lips that spoil the ruby's praise,
From eyes that mock the diamond's blaze:
Whence comes my woe, as freely own;
Ah, me! 'twas from a heart like stone.

The blushing cheek speaks modest mind,
The lips befitting words most kind,
The eye does tempt to love's desire,
And seems to say 'tis Cupid's fire;
Yet all so fair but speak my moan,
Sith naught doth say the heart of stone.

Why thus, my love, so kind bespeak
Sweet eye, sweet lip, sweet blushing cheek—
Yet not a heart to save my pain?
Oh, Venus! take thy gifts again!
Make not so fair to cause our moan,
Or make a heart that's like our own.

# Edward Vere, Earl of Oxford.

[BORN 1534.  DIED 1604.]

## A RENUNCIATION.

IF women could be fair, and yet not fond,
　Or that their love were firm, not fickle still,
　I would not marvel that they make men bond
　　By service long to purchase their good-will;
But when I see how frail those creatures are,
I muse that men forget themselves so far.

To mark the choice they make, and how they change,
　How oft from Phœbus they do flee to Pan;
Unsettled still, like haggards wild they range,
　These gentle birds that fly from man to man;
Who would not scorn and shake them from the fist,
And let them fly, fair fools, which way they list?

Yet for disport we fawn and flatter both,
　To pass the time when nothing else can please,
And train them to our lure with subtle oath,
　Till, weary of their wiles, ourselves we ease;
And then we say when we their fancy try,
To play with fools, O what a fool was I!

# Christopher Marlowe.

[Born 1552 (?). Died 1593.]

---

## The Passionate Shepherd.

COME live with me, and be my love,
And we will all the pleasures prove
That vallies, groves, and hills and fields,
The woods or steepy mountains yields.

And we will sit upon the rocks,
Seeing the shepherds feed their flocks,
By shallow rivers, to whose falls
Melodious birds sing madrigals.

And I will make thee beds of roses,
And a thousand fragrant posies ;
A cap of flowers and a kirtle,
Embroidered o'er with leaves of myrtle.

A gown made of the finest wool,
Which from our pretty lambs we pull ;
Fair lined slippers for the cold,
With buckles of the purest gold.

A belt of straw and ivy buds,
With coral clasps and amber studs ;
And if these pleasures thee may move,
Come live with me, and be my love.

The shepherd swains shall dance and sing,
For thy delight, each May morning ;
If these delights thy mind may move,
Then live with me and be my love.

# Sir Walter Raleigh.

[Born 1552.   Died 1618.]

### The Nymph's Reply.

IF all the world and love were young,
And truth on every shepherd's tongue,
These pleasures might my passion move
To live with thee, and be thy love.

But fading flowers in every field,
To winter floods their treasures yield ;
A honeyed tongue, a heart of gall,
Is Fancy's spring, but Sorrow's fall.

Thy gown, thy shoes, thy beds of roses,
Thy cap, thy kirtle, and thy posies,
Are all soon withered, broke, forgotten,
In Folly ripe, in Reason rotten.

Thy belt of straw and ivy buds,
Thy coral clasps and amber studs,
Can me with no enticements move
To live with thee, and be thy love.

But could youth last, could Love still breed,
Had Joy no date, had Age no need;
Then those delights my mind might move,
To live with thee, and be thy love.

# Edmund Spenser.

[Born 1553.   Died 1598.]

## SONNET.

YE tradeful merchants! that with weary toil
Do seek most precious things to make
your gain,
And both the Indies of their treasure spoil,
What needeth you to seek so far in
vain?

For, lo! my love doth in herself contain
All this world's riches that may far be found;
If sapphires, lo! her eyes be sapphires plain;
If rubies, lo! her lips be rubies sound;

If pearls, her teeth be pearls, both pure and round,
If ivory, her forehead ivory ween;
If gold, her locks are finest gold on ground;
If silver, her fair hands are silver sheen:

But that which fairest is, but few behold,
Her mind, adorned with virtues manifold.

# Sir Philip Sidney.

[BORN 1554.   DIED 1586.]

## A DITTY.

MY true love hath my heart, and I have his,
  By just exchange, one to the other given:
I hold his dear, and mine he cannot miss,
  There never was a better bargain driven:
My true love hath my heart, and I have his.

His heart in me keeps him and me in one,
  My heart in him his thoughts and senses guides:
He loves my heart, for once it was his own,
  I cherish his because in me it bides:
My true love hath my heart, and I have his.

# John Lylye.

[Born 1554.   Died 1600.]

## Cupid and Campaspe.

CUPID and my Campaspe played
At cards for kisses; Cupid paid:
He stakes his quiver, bow, and arrows,
His mother's dove, and team of sparrows;
Loses them too; then down he throws
The coral of his lip, the rose
Growing on's cheek (but none knows how):
With these, the crystal of his brow,
And then the dimple on his chin;
All these did my Campaspe win:
At last he set her both his eyes—
She won, and Cupid blind did rise.
   O Love! has she done this to thee?
   What shall, alas! become of me?

2

# Nicholas Breton.

[Born 1555.   Died 16 –.]

---

### Phillida and Corydon.

IN the merry month of May,
In a morn by break of day,
With a troop of damsels playing,
Forth I went—forsooth, a Maying.

Where anon by a wood side,
Where as May was in his pride,
I espied all alone,
Phillida and Corydon.

Much ado there was, God wot ;
He would love and she would not.
She said, never man was true ;
He says, none was false to you.

He said, he had loved her long ;
She says, love should have no wrong.
Corydon would kiss her then ;
She says, maids must kiss no men

Till they do for good and all—
When she made the shepherd call
All the heavens to witness truth,
Never loved a truer youth.

Then with many a pretty oath,
Yea and nay, and faith and troth ;
Such as silly shepherds use
When they will not love abuse ;

Love that had been long deluded,
Was with kisses sweet concluded ;
And Phillida, with garlands gay,
Was made the lady of the May.

# Thomas Lodge.

[Born 1556.   Died 1625.]

### Rosalind's Complaint.

LOVE in my bosom, like a bee,
    Doth suck his sweet;
Now with his wings he plays with me,
    Now with his feet;
Within mine eyes he makes his nest,
His bed amidst my tender breast;
My kisses are his daily feast,
And yet he robs me of my rest:
    Ah! wanton, will you?

And if I sleep, then pierceth he
    With pretty slight,
And makes his pillow of my knee
    The live-long night;
Strike I the lute, he tunes the string,
He music plays, if I but sing;
He lends me every lovely thing,
Yet cruel, he my heart doth sting:
    Ah! wanton, will you?

Else I with roses every day
  Will whip you hence,
And bind you when you long to play,
  For your offence ;
I'll shut my eyes to keep you in,
I'll make you fast it for your sin,
I'll count your power not worth a pin ;
Alas ! what hereby shall I win,
  If he gainsay me ?

What if I beat the wanton boy
  With many a rod,
He will repay me with annoy,
  Because a god ;
Then sit thou softly on my knee,
And let thy bower my bosom be ;
Lurk in my eyes, I like of thee,
O Cupid ! so thou pity me ;
  Spare not, but play thee.

# Robert Greene.

[Born 1560(?).   Died 1592.]

---

### MELICERTUS'S DESCRIPTION.

TUNE on, my pipe, the praises of my love,
   And midst thy oaten harmony* recount
   How fair she is that makes my music mount,
And every string of my heart's harp to move.

Shall I compare her form unto the sphere,
   Whence sun-bright Venus vaunts her silver shine?
   Ah, more than that by just compare is thine,
Whose crystal looks the cloudy heavens do clear!

How oft have I descending Titan seen
   His burning locks quench in the sea-queen's lap,
   And beauteous Thetis his red body wrap
In watery robes, as he her lord had been.

---

* In the old poets this word is frequently used in the sense of melody.

When as my nymph, impatient of the night,
   Bade bright Arcturus with his train give place,
   Whiles she led forth the day with her fair face,
And lent each star a more than Delian light.

Not Jove nor Nature, should they both agree
   To make a woman of the firmament
   Of his mixed purity, could not* invent
A sky-born form so beautiful as she.

---

* *Sic.*

# Samuel Danyell.

[BORN 1562.   DIED 1619.]

## A Character of Love.

OVE is a sickness full of woes,
  All remedies refusing,
A plant that with most cutting grows,
  Most barren with best using.
        Why so?
If we enjoy it, soon it dies;
If not enjoyed, it sighing cries
        Hey ho!

Love is a torment of the mind,
  A tempest everlasting,
  A heaven has made it of a kind,
Not well;—nor full, nor fasting.
        Why so?
If we enjoy it, soon it dies;
If not enjoyed, it sighing cries
        Hey ho!

## To Delia.

NTO the boundless ocean of thy beauty,
    Runs this poor river, charged with streams
        of zeal,
    Returning thee the tribute of my duty,
      Which here my love, my youth, my plaints
        reveal.
Here I unclasp the book of my charged soul,
    Where I have cast th' accounts of all my care;
Here have I summed my sighs; here I enrol
    How they were spent for thee; look what they are.
Look on the dear expenses of my youth,
    And see how just I reckon with thine eyes:
Examine well thy beauty with my truth;
    And cross my cares, ere greater cares arise.
Read it, sweet maid, though it be done but slightly;
Who can show all his love, doth love but lightly.

# Henry Constable.

[Born 1562 (?).    Died 1604 (?).]

## DIAPHENIA.

DIAPHENIA, like the daffadoundilly,
White as the sun, fair as the lily,
  Heigh-ho, how I do love thee!
  I do love thee as my lambs
  Are beloved of their dams;
How blest I were if thou wouldst prove me.

Diaphenia, like the spreading roses,
That in thy sweets all sweets encloses,
  Fair sweet, how I do love thee!
  I do love thee as each flower
  Loves the sun's life-giving power;
For dead, thy breath to life might move me.

Diaphenia, like to all things blessed,
When all thy praises are expressed,
  Dear joy, how I do love thee!
  As the birds do love the spring,
  Or the bees their careful king:
Then in requite, sweet virgin, love me!

# Joshua Sylvester.

[Born 1563.   Died 1618.]

## Love's Omnipresence.

WERE I as base as is the lowly plain,
  And you, my Love, as high as heaven above,
  Yet should the thoughts of me, your humble
        swain,
  Ascend to heaven, in honor of my Love.

Were I as high as heaven above the plain,
  And you, my Love, as humble and as low
As are the deepest bottoms of the main,
  Wheresoe'er you were, with you my love should go.

Were you the earth, dear Love, and I the skies,
  My love should shine on you like to the sun,
And look upon you with ten thousand eyes
  Till heaven waxed blind, and till the world were
        done.

Wheresoe'er I am, below, or else above you,
Wheresoe'er you are, my heart shall truly love you.

# Michael Drayton.

[Born 1563. Died 1631.]

---

### LOVE'S FAREWELL.

SINCE there's no help, come let us kiss and
    part,—
    Nay, I have done, you get no more oi
    me ;
And I am glad, yea glad with all my heart,
    That thus so cleanly I myself can free ;

Shake hands forever, cancel all our vows,
    And when we meet at any time again,
Be it not seen in either of our brows
    That we one jot of former love retain.

Now at the last gasp of love's latest breath,
    When his pulse failing, passion speechless lies
When faith is kneeling by his bed of death,
    And innocence is closing up his eyes,

—Now if thou wouldst, when all have given him
    over,
From death to life thou might'st him yet recover.

# William Shakspeare.

[Born 1564.   Died 1616.]

## "Take, oh, take those lips away." *

TAKE, oh, take those lips away,
    That so sweetly were forsworn!
And those eyes, the break of day,
    Lights that do mislead the morn;
But my kisses bring again,
Seals of love, but sealed in vain.

Hide, oh, hide those hills of snow,
    Which thy frozen bosom bears!
On whose tops the pinks that grow
    Are of those that April wears;
But first set my poor heart free,
Bound in those icy chains by thee.

---

* The authorship of the above is an unsettled question. The first stanza will be found in *Measure for Measure;* and the idea contained in "Seals of love, but sealed in vain," is to be found in one of Shakspeare's sonnets, and in *Venus and Adonis.* Both stanzas are in one of Beaumont and Fletcher's plays. The probability is that the first stanza is by Shakspeare, and the next by Fletcher.

### A DESCRIPTION.

ONE of her hands one of her cheeks lay under,
    Cozening the pillow of a lawful kiss, .
    Which therefore swelled, and seemed to part
        asunder,
    As angry to be robbed of such a bliss ,
The one looked pale, and for revenge did long,
While th' other blushed, 'cause it had done the wrong.

Out of the bed the other fair hand was
    On a green satin quilt, whose perfect white
Looked like a daisy in a field of grass,
    And showed like unmelt snow unto the sight.*

---

* Sir John Suckling completed this unfinished poem, but the addition is an inferior one.

## LOVE'S PERJURIES.

N a day, alack the day!
Love, whose month is ever May,
Spied a blossom passing fair
Playing in the wanton air:
Through the velvet leaves the wind
All unseen 'gan passage find;
That the lover, sick to death,
Wished himself the heaven's breath.
Air, quoth he, thy cheeks may blow;
Air, would I might triumph so!
But, alack, my hand is sworn
Ne'er to pluck thee from thy thorn:
Vow, alack for youth unmeet;
Youth so apt to pluck a sweet.
Do not call it sin in me
That I am forsworn for thee:
Thou for whom e'en Jove would swear
Juno but an Ethiope were,
And deny himself for Jove,
Turning mortal for thy love.

## TRUE LOVE.

LET me not to the marriage of true minds
    Admit impediments.   Love is not love
Which alters when it alteration finds,
    Or bends with the remover to remove :—

O no ! it is an ever-fixed mark
    That looks on tempests, and is never shaken ;
It is the star to every wandering barque
    Whose worth's unknown, although his height be
      taken.

Love's not time's fool, though rosy lips and cheeks
    Within his bending sickle's compass come ;
Love alters not with his brief hours and weeks,
    But bears it out even to the edge of doom :—

If this be error, and upon me proved,
I never writ, nor no man ever loved.

### ABSENCE.

BEING your slave, what should I do but tend
    Upon the hours and time of your desire?
    I have no precious time at all to spend,
    Nor services to do, till you require;

Nor dare I chide the world-without-end hour
    Whilst I, my sovereign, watch the clock for
        you,
Nor think the bitterness of absence sour
    When you have bid your servant once adieu:

Nor dare I question with my jealous thought
    Where you may be, or your affairs suppose,
But, like a sad slave, stay and think of naught
    Save, where you are, how happy you make those:

So true a fool is love, that in your will,
Though you do any thing, he thinks no ill.

### THE UNCHANGEABLE.

NEVER say that I was false of heart,
   Though absence seemed my flame to qualify:
As easy might I from myself depart
   As from my soul, which in thy breast doth
     lie.

This is my home of love; if I have ranged,
   Like him that travels, I return again,
Just with the time, not with the time exchanged,
   So that myself bring water for my stain.

Never believe, though in my nature reigned
   All frailties that besiege all kinds of blood,
That it could so preposterously be stained
   To leave for nothing all thy sum of good:

For nothing this wide universe I call,
Save thou, my rose: in it thou art my all.

# Richard Barnefield.

[Contemporary with SHAKESPEARE.   Birth uncertain.]

---

### THE NIGHTINGALE.

AS it fell upon a day
In the merry month of May,
Sitting in a pleasant shade
Which a grove of myrtles made,
Beasts did leap and birds did sing,
Trees did grow and plants did spring,
Every thing did banish moan
Save the nightingale alone.
She, poor bird, as all forlorn,
Leaned her breast against a thorn,
And there sung the dolefullest ditty
That to hear it was great pity.
Fie, fie, fie, now would she cry;
Tereu, tereu, by and by:
That to hear her so complain
Scarce I could from tears refrain;
For her griefs so lively shown
Made me think upon mine own.

—Ah, thought I, thou mourn'st in vain,
None takes pity on thy pain:
Senseless trees, they cannot hear thee,
Ruthless beasts, they will not cheer thee ;
King Pandion, he is dead,
All thy friends are lapped in lead:
All thy fellow-birds do sing
Careless of thy sorrowing:
Even so, poor bird, like thee
None alive will pity me.

# Sir Henry Wotton.

[Born 1568.    Died 1639.]

---

## "You Meaner Beauties."*

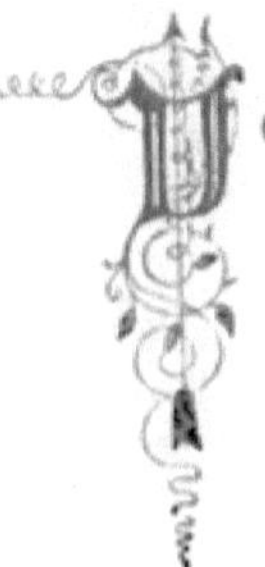

YOU meaner beauties of the night
  That poorly satisfy our eyes,
More by your number than your light ;
  You common people of the skies,
  What are you when the moon shall rise ?

Ye violets that first appear
  By your pure purple mantles known,
Like the proud virgins of the year,
  As if the Spring were all your own ;
  What are you when the rose is blown ?

Ye curious chaunters of the wood,
  That warble forth dame Nature's lays,

---

* Chambers attributes this song to Lord Darnley, king consort of Mary, queen of Scots.  There appears no doubt, after investigation, that it was written by Wotton, and was addressed to the Queen of Bohemia, daughter of James I.

Thinking your passion understood
   By your weak accents—what's your praise,
   When Philomel her voice shall raise?

So when my mistress shall be seen,
   In sweetness of her looks and mind :
By virtue first, then choice a queen,
   Tell me if she was not designed
   Th' eclipse and glory of her kind?

# Sir Robert Aytoun.

[Born 1570.    Died 1638.]

## WOMAN'S INCONSTANCY.

I LOVED thee once, I'll love no more,
    Thine be the grief, as is the blame;
Thou art not what thou wert before,
    What reason I should be the same?
He that can love, unloved again,
Hath better store of love than brain;
God send me love my debts to pay,
While unthrifts fool their love away.

Nothing could have my love o'erthrown,
    If thou hadst still continued mine;
Yea, if thou hadst remained thy own,
    I might perchance have yet been thine:
But thou thy freedom did recall,
That it thou might elsewhere enthral;
And then how could I but disdain,
A captive's captive to remain?

When new desires had conquered thee,
   And changed the object of thy will ;
It had been lethargy in me,
   Not constancy, to love thee still.
Yea, it had been a sin to go
And prostitute affection so ;
Since we are taught our prayers to say,
To such as must to others pray.

Yet do thou glory in thy choice,
   Thy choice of his good fortune boast ;
I'll neither grieve nor yet rejoice,
   To see him gain what I have lost :
The height of my disdain shall be,
To laugh at him, to blush for thee,
To love thee still, but go no more
A begging at a beggar's door.

----

### "I DO CONFESS."

I DO confess thou'rt smooth and fair,
   And I might have gone near to love thee,
Had I not found the slightest prayer
   That lips can speak had power to move thee ;
But I can let thee now alone,
   As worthy to be loved by none.

I do confess thee sweet, but find
  Thee such an unthrift of thy sweets,
Thy favours are but like the wind
  That kisseth every thing it meets :
And since thou canst with more than one,
Thou'rt worthy to be kissed by none.

The morning rose that untouched stands,
  Armed with her briers, doth sweetly smell,
But plucked and strained through ruder hands
  Her sweets no longer with her dwell,
Her scent and beauty both are gone,
And leaves fall from her one by one.

Such fate ere long will thee betide,
  When thou hast handled been awhile—
Like sere flowers to be thrown aside ;
  And I shall sigh, while some will smile,
To see thy love to every one
Hath caused thee to be loved by none.

3

# John Donne.

[Born 1573.   Died 1631.]

---

## The Message.

SEND home my long-strayed eyes to me,
Which, oh! too long have dwelt on thee,
But if they there have learned such ill,
Such forced fashions
And false passions,
That they be
Made by thee
Fit for no good sight, keep them still.

Send home my harmless heart again,
Which no unworthy thought could stain;
But if it be taught by thine
To make jestings
Of protestings,
And break both
Word and oath,
Keep it still, 'tis none of mine.

Yet send me back my heart and eyes,
That I may know and see thy lies,
And may joy and laugh when thou
    Art in anguish
    And dost languish
      For some one
      That will none,
Or prove false as thou dost now.

---

## The Prohibition.

TAKE heed of loving me—
At least remember I forbade it thee ;
Not that I shall repair my unthrifty waste
    Of breath and blood upon thy sighs and tears.
By being to thee then what to me thou wast ;
    But so great joy our life at once outwears ;
Then, lest thy love by my death frustrate be,
If thou love me, take heed of loving me.

    Take heed of hating me,
Or too much triumph in the victory ;
Not that I shall be mine own officer,
    And hate with hate again retaliate ;

But thou wilt lose the style of Conqueror,
　If I, thy conquest, perish by thy hate;
Then, lest my being nothing lessen thee,
If thou hate me, take heed of hating me.


　　Yet love and hate me too,
So these extremes shall ne'er their office do;
Love me, that I may die the gentler way;
　Hate me, because thy love's too great for me·
Or let these two themselves, not me, decay;
　So shall I live thy stage, not triumph be:
Then lest thy love thou hate, and me undo,
O let me live, yet love and hate me too.

# Ben Jonson.

[Born 1574.   Died 1637.]

---

### "Drink to Me only."

DRINK to me only with thine eyes,
  And I will pledge with mine;
Or leave a kiss but in the cup,
  And I'll not look for wine.
The thirst that from my soul doth rise
  Doth ask a drink divine;
But might I of Jove's nectar sip,
  I would not change for thine.

I sent thee late a rosy wreath,
  Not so much honouring thee,
As giving it a hope, that there
  It would not withered be,
But thou thereon didst only breathe,
  And sent it back to me;
Since then, it grows and smells, I swear,
  Not of itself, but thee.

# John Fletcher.

[Born 1576.  Died 1625.]

## SONG.

DEAREST! do not thou delay me,
    Since thou know'st I must be gone;
Wind and tide, 'tis thought, doth stay me,
    But 'tis wind that must be blown
From that breath, whose native smell
Indian odours far excel.

Oh, then speak, thou fairest fair!
    Kill not him that vows to serve thee;
But perfume this neighbouring air,
    Else dull silence sure will starve me;
'Tis a word that's quickly spoken,
Which being restrained, a heart is broken.

# Thomas Carew.

[Born 1580(?).   Died 1639.]

---

## MEDIOCRITY IN LOVE REJECTED.

GIVE me more love, or more disdain;
  The torrid or the frozen zone
Bring equal ease unto my pain,
  The temperate affords me none;
Either extreme of love or hate
Is sweeter than a calm estate.

Give me a storm; if it be love,
  Like Danae in that golden shower,
I swim in pleasure; if it prove
  Disdain, that torrent will devour
My vulture-hopes; and he's possessed
Of heaven that's but from hell released;
Then crown my joys or cure my pain;
Give me more love, or more disdain.

## SONG.

H E that loves a rosy cheek,
　　Or a coral lip admires,
Or from star-like eyes doth seek
　　Fuel to maintain its fires ;
As old Time makes these decay,
So his flames must waste away.

But a smooth and stedfast mind,
　　Gentle thoughts and calm desires,
Hearts with equal love combined,
　　Kindle never-dying fires ;
Where these are not, I despise
Lovely cheeks, or lips, or eyes.

# William Alexander, Earl of Sterling.

[Born 1580.  Died 1640.]

## To Aurora.

IF thou knew'st how thou thyself dost harm,
   And dost prejudge thy bliss, and spoil my
      rest ;
   Then thou wouldst melt the ice out of thy
      breast,
   And thy relenting heart would kindly warm.

O if thy pride did not our joys control,
   What world of loving wonders shouldst thou see !
   For if I saw thee once transformed in me,
Then in thy bosom I would pour my soul ;

Then all my thoughts should in thy visage shine,
   And if that aught mischanced thou shouldst not moan
   Nor bear the burthen of thy griefs alone ;
No, I would have my share in what were thine :

And whilst we thus should make our sorrows one,
This happy harmony would make them none.

3*

# William Drummond.

[Born 1585.　Died 1649.]

---

### Summons to Love.

PHŒBUS, arise !
　　And paint the sable skies
　　With azure, white, and red :
Rouse Memnon's mother from her Tithon's bed,
That she may thy career with roses spread :
The nightingales thy coming each where sing :
　　Make an eternal spring !
Give life to this dark world which lieth dead ;
　　Spread forth thy golden hair
In larger locks than thou wast wont before,
　　And emperor-like decore
With diadem of pearl thy temples fair :
　　Chase hence the ugly night,
Which serves but to make dear thy glorious light.

　　—This is that happy morn,
　　　That day, long wished day
　　　Of all my life so dark
(If cruel stars have not my ruin sworn

And fates my hopes betray),
 Which, purely white, deserves
An everlasting diamond should it mark.
This is the morn should bring unto this grove
My Love, to hear and recompense my love.
  Fair king, who all preserves,
  But show thy blushing beams,
   And thou two sweeter eyes
Shalt see than those which by Peneus' streams
   Did once thy heart surprise.
Now, Flora, deck thyself in fairest guise :
   If that ye winds would hear
 A voice surpassing far Amphion's lyre,
   Your furious chiding stay ;
   Let Zephyr only breathe,
  And with her tresses play.
  —The winds all silent are,
  And Phœbus in his chair
  Ensaffroning sea and air
  Makes vanish every star :
  Night, like a drunkard, reels
Beyond the hills, to show his flaming wheels :
The fields with flowers are decked in every hue,
The clouds with orient gold spangle their blue ;
  Here is the pleasant place—
And nothing wanting is, save She, alas !

## The Quality of a Kiss.

THE kiss, with so much strife
 Which late I got (sweet heart),
 Was it a sign of death, or was it life?
 Of life it could not be,
For I by it did sigh my soul to thee:
Nor was it death—death doth no joy impart.
Thou silent stand'st, ah! what didst thou bequeath,
A dying life to me, or living death?

---

## Sleeping Beauty.

SIGHT too dearly bought:
 She sleeps, and though those eyes
 Which lighten Cupid's sighs
 Be closed, yet such a grace
 Environeth that place,
That I through wonder to grow faint am brought:
Suns, if eclipsed, you have such power divine,
What power have I t'endure you when you shine?

# Richard Allison.

[From " An Houre's Recreation in Musicke."—1606.]

---

"THERE IS A GARDEN IN HER FACE."

THERE is a garden in her face,
    Where roses and white lilies grow ;
A heavenly paradise is that place,
    Wherein all pleasant fruits do grow ;
There cherries grow that none may buy,
Till cherry-ripe themselves do cry.

Those cherries fairly do inclose
    Of orient pearl a double row,
Which when her lovely laughter shows,
    They look like rose-buds filled with snow ;
Yet them no peer nor prince may buy,
Till cherry-ripe themselves do cry.*

---

* It is probable that Herrick's Song of " Cherry Ripe" was suggested
by this stanza.

Her eyes like angels watch them still,
  Her brows like bended bows do stand,
Threatening with piercing frowns to kill
  All that approach with eye or hand
Those sacred cherries to come nigh,
Till cherry-ripe themselves do cry.

# Giles Fletcher.

[Born 1588.   Died 1623.]

### Panglory's Wooing Song.

LOVE is the blossom where there blows
Every thing that lives or grows;
Love doth make the heavens to move,
And the sun doth burn in love:
Love, the strong and weak doth yoke,
And makes the ivy climb the oak,
Under whose shadows, lions wild,
Softened by love grow tame and mild.
Love, no med'cine can appease;
He burns the fishes in the seas;
Not all the skill his wounds can staunch;
Not all the sea his thirst can quench.
Love did make the bloody spear
Once a leafy coat to wear,
While in his leaves there shrouded lay
Sweet birds, for love that sing and play;
And of all love's joyful flame
I the bud and blossom am.
    Only bend thy knee to me,
    Thy wooing shall my winning be.

See, see  the flowers that below
Now freshly as the morning blow,
And of all, the virgin rose,
That as bright Aurora shows;
How they all unleaved die
Losing their virginity ;
Like unto a summer shade,
But now born, and now they fade,
Every thing doth pass away ;
There is danger in delay.
Come, come, gather then the rose ;
Gather it, or it you lose.
All the sand of Tagus' shore,
In my bosom casts its ore :
All the valleys' swimming corn
To my house is yearly borne :
Every grape of every vine
Is gladly bruised to make me wine ;
While ten thousand kings, as proud
To carry up my train, have bowed,
And a world of ladies send me
From my chamber to attend me :
All the stars in heaven that shine,
And ten thousand more are mine.
   Only bend thy knee to me,
    Thy wooing shall thy winning be.

# George Wither.

[Born 1588.  Died 1667.]

---

"SHALL I, WASTING IN DESPAIR."

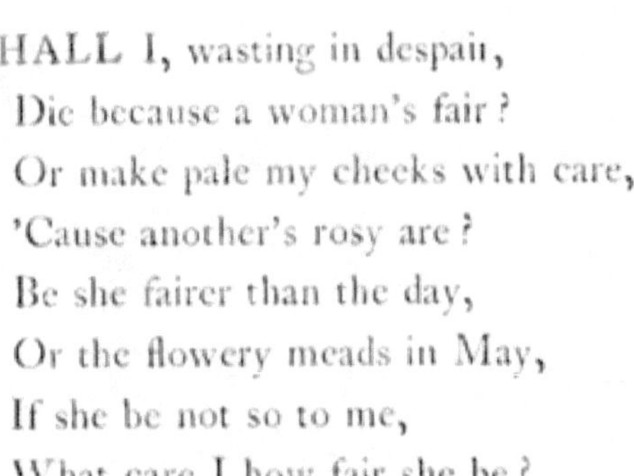

SHALL I, wasting in despair,
Die because a woman's fair?
Or make pale my cheeks with care,
'Cause another's rosy are?
Be she fairer than the day,
Or the flowery meads in May,
If she be not so to me,
What care I how fair she be?

Should my heart be grieved or pined
'Cause I see a woman kind?
Or a well-disposed nature
Joined with a lovely feature?
Be she meeker, kinder, than
Turtle-dove or pelican,
If she be not so to me,
What care I how kind she be?

Shall a woman's virtues move
Me to perish for her love?
Or, her well-deservings known,
Make me quite forget my own?
Be she with that goodness blest
Which may gain her name of best,
If she be not such to me,
What care I how good she be?

'Cause her fortune seems too high,
Shall I play the fool and die?
Those that bear a noble mind,
Where they want of riches find,
Think what with them they would do,
That without them dare to woo;
And unless that mind I see,
What care I how great she be?

Great, or good, or kind, or fair,
I will ne'er the more despair:
If she love me, this believe,
I will die ere she shall grieve:
If she slight me when I woo,
I can scorn and let her go:
For, if she be not for me,
What care I for whom she be?

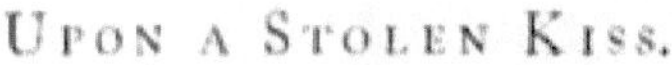

## Upon a Stolen Kiss.

OW gentle sleep hath closed up those eyes
   Which, waking, kept my boldest thoughts
      in awe ;
And free access unto that sweet lip lies,
   From whence I long the rosy breath to
      draw.
Methinks no wrong it were, if I should steal
   From those two melting rubies, one poor kiss ;
None sees the theft that would the theft reveal,
   Nor rob I her of aught what she can miss :
Nay, should I twenty kisses take away,
   There would be little sign I would do so ;
Why then should I this robbery delay ?
   Oh ! she may wake, and therewith angry grow !
Well, if she do, I'll back restore that one,
And twenty hundred thousand more for loan.

# William Browne.

[Born 1590.   Died 1645.]

---

"Welcome, Welcome, do I sing."

WELCOME, welcome, do I sing,
Far more welcome than the spring,
He that parteth from you never,
Shall enjoy a spring forever.

Love, that to the voice is near,
  Breaking from your ivory pale,
Need not walk abroad to hear
  The delightful nightingale.
    Welcome, welcome, then I sing, &c.

Love, that looks still on your eyes,
  Though the winter have begun
To benumb our arteries,
  Shall not want the summer's sun.
    Welcome, welcome, then I sing, &c.

Love, that still may see your cheeks,
  Where all rareness still reposes,

'Tis a fool, if e'er he seeks
  Other lilies, other roses.
    Welcome, welcome, then I sing, &c.


Love, to whom your soft lip yields,
  And perceives your breath in kissing,
All the odors of the fields
  Never, never shall be missing.
    Welcome, welcome, then I sing, &c.


Love, that question would anew
  What fair Eden was of old,
Let him rightly study you,
  And a brief of that behold.
    Welcome, welcome, then I sing, &c.

----

### SONG.

HALL I tell you whom I love?
  Hearken then awhile to me;
And if such a woman prove
  As I now shall verify;
Be assured, 'tis she or none
That I love, and love alone.

Nature did her so much right,
  As she scorns the help of art.
In as many virtues dight
  As e'er yet embraced a heart.
So much good so truly tried,
Some for less were deified.

Wit she hath, without desire
  To make known how much she hath;
And her anger flames no higher
  Than may fitly sweeten wrath.
Full of pity as may be,
Though perhaps not so to me.

Reason masters every sense,
  And her virtues grace her birth;
Lovely as all excellence,
  Modest in her most of mirth:
Likelihood enough to prove
Only worth would kindle love.

Such she is, and if you know
  Such a one as I have sung;
Be she brown, or fair, or so
  That she be but somewhile young;
Be assured, 'tis she or none
That I love, and love alone.

# Henry King, Bishop of Chichester.

[Born 1591. Died 1669.]

## "TELL ME NO MORE."

TELL me no more how fair she is;
   I have no mind to hear
The story of that distant bliss
   I never shall come near:
By sad experience I have found
That her perfection is my wound.

And tell me not how fond I am
   To tempt my daring fate,
From whence no triumph ever came
   But to repent too late:
There is some hope ere long I may
In silence dote myself away.

I ask no pity, Love, from thee,
   Nor will thy justice blame,—
So that thou wilt not envy me
   The glory of my flame,
Which crowns my heart whene'er it dies,
In that it falls her sacrifice.

# Robert Herrick.

[BORN 1591.   DIED 1671 (?).]

---

### THE KISS: A DIALOGUE.

1.

AMONG thy fancies tell me this :
What is the thing we call a kiss ?—
2. I shall resolve ye what it is :

It is a creature born and bred
Between the lips, all cherry red ;
By love and warm desires fed ;
*Chor.* And makes more soft the bridal bed.

2. It is an active flame, that flies
First to the babies of the eyes,
And charms them there with lullabies ;
*Chor.* And stills the bride too when she cries.

Then to the chin, the cheek, the ear,
It frisks and flies ; now here, now there ;
'Tis now far off, and then 'tis near ;
*Chor.* And here, and there, and everywhere.

1. Has it a speaking virtue?—2. Yes.
1. How speaks it, say?—2. Do you but this,
    Part your joined lips, then speaks your kiss;
*Chor.* And this love's sweetest language is.


1. Has it a body?—2. Ay, and wings,
    With thousand rare encolorings;
    And as it flies, it gently sings,
*Chor.* Love honey yields, but never stings.

———

### "Go, Happy Rose."

GO, happy Rose, and, interwove
With other flowers, bind my love.
    Tell her, too, she must not be
    Longer flowing, longer free,
    That so oft hath fettered me.


Say, if she's fretful, I have bands
Of pearl and gold to bind her hands;
    Tell her, if she struggle still,
    I have myrtle rods at will,
    For to tame, though not to kill.


Take then my blessing thus, and go,
And tell her this,—but do not so!

Lest a handsome anger fly,
Like a lightning from her eye,
And burn thee up, as well as I.

———

## TO ANTHEA,

### WHO MAY COMMAND HIM ANY THING.

BID me to live, and I will live
  Thy Protestant to be:
Or bid me love, and I will give
  A loving heart to thee.

A heart as soft, a heart as kind,
  A heart as sound and free
As in the whole world thou canst find,
  That heart I'll give to thee.

Bid that heart stay, and it will stay,
  To honor thy decree:
Or bid it languish quite away,
  And 't shall do so for thee.

Bid me to weep, and I will weep
  While I have eyes to see:
And having none, yet I will keep
  A heart to weep for thee.

Bid me despair, and I'll despair,
　　Under that cypress-tree :
Or bid me die, and I will dare
　　E'en Death, to die for thee.

Thou art my life, my love, my heart,
　　The very eyes of me,
And hast command of every part,
　　To live and die for thee.

---

## To Dianeme.

SWEET, be not proud of those two eyes
Which star-like sparkle in their skies;
Nor be you proud, that you can see
All hearts your captives; yours yet free:
Be you not proud of that rich hair
Which wantons with the love-sick air;
Whenas that ruby which you wear,
Sunk from the tip of your soft ear,
Will last to be a precious stone
When all your world of beauty's gone.

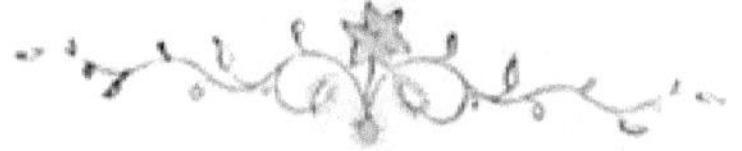

# Thomas Heywood.

[Date of birth and death uncertain.   Flourished from 1596 to 1640.]

---

### Good-Morrow.

PACK clouds away, and welcome day,
  With night we banish sorrow;
Sweet air blow soft, mount larks aloft,
  To give my love Good-morrow!

Wings from the wind to please her mind,
  Notes from the lark I'll borrow;
Bird prune thy wing, nightingale sing,
  To give my love Good-morrow!

Wake from thy nest, robin red-breast,
  Sing birds in every furrow,
And from each hill let music shrill
  Give my fair love Good-morrow!

Blackbird and thrush, in every bush,
  Stare, linnet, and cock-sparrow,
You pretty elves among yourselves,
  Sing my fair love Good-morrow!

## "Ye Little Birds."

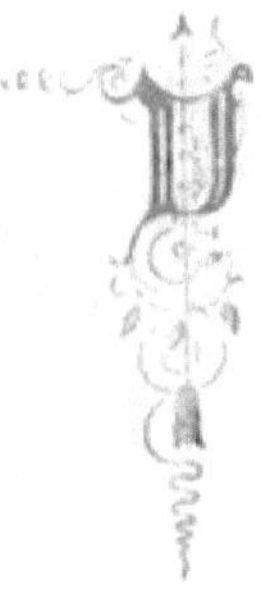

YE little birds that sit and sing
    Amidst the shady vallies,
And see how Phillis sweetly walks
    Within her garden alleys;
Go, pretty birds, about her bower,
Sing, pretty birds, she may not lower,
Ah, me! methinks I see her frown,—
    Ye pretty wantons, warble.


Go tell her through your chirping bills
    As you by me are bidden,
To her is only known my love,
    Which from the world is hidden.
Go, pretty birds, and tell her so,
See that your notes strain not too low,
For still methinks I see her frown,—
    Ye pretty wantons, warble.


Go tune your voices' harmony,
    And sing I am her lover;
Strain loud and sweet, that every note
    With sweet content may move her;
And she that hath the sweetest voice,
Tell her I will not change my choice;

Yet still methinks I see her frown, —
   Ye pretty wantons, warble.

O fly, make haste,—see, see, she falls
   Into a pretty slumber;
Sing round about her rosy bed,
   That waking she may wonder.
Sing to her 'tis her lover true
That sendeth love by you and you,
And when you hear her kind reply,
   Return with pleasant warblings.

# William Strode.

[Born 1600.   Died 1644.]

### "My Love and I."

M Y love and I for kisses played;
 She would keep stakes, I was content;
But when I won she would be paid,
 This made me ask her what she meant;
Nay, since I see (quoth she) you wrangle in vain,
Take your own kisses, give me mine again.

# William Habington.

[BORN 1605.    DIED 1654.]

## CASTARA.

IKE the violet which, alone,
  Prospers in some happy shade,
My Castara lives unknown,
  To no looser eye betrayed,
For she's to herself untrue
Who delights i' th' public view.

Such is her beauty as no arts
  Have enriched with borrowed grace ;
Her high birth no pride imparts,
  For she blushes in her place.
Folly boasts a glorious blood,
She is noblest being good.

*      *      *      *      *

She her throne makes reason climb,
  While wild passions captive lie :
And each article of time
  Her pure thoughts to heaven fly :
All her vows religious be,
And her love she vows to me.

# Sir William Davenant.

[Born 1605.    Died 1668.]

### SONG.

THE lark now leaves his watery nest,
    And climbing shakes his dewy wings;
He takes his window for the east,
    And to implore your light, he sings,—
Awake, awake, the morn will never rise,
Till she can dress her beauty by your eyes.

The merchant bows unto the seaman's star,
    The ploughman from the sun his season takes;
But still the lover wonders what they are
    Who look for day before his mistress wakes:
Awake, awake, break through your veils of lawn!
Then draw your curtains, and begin the dawn.

# Edmund Waller.

[Born 1605.   Died 1687.]

### On a Girdle.

THAT which her slender waist confined
Shall now my joyful temples bind :
No monarch but would give his crown
His arms might do what this has done.

It was my heaven's extremest sphere,
The pale which held that lovely dear :
My joy, my grief, my hope, my love,
Did all within this circle move.

A narrow compass ! and yet there
Dwelt all that's good, and all that's fair :
Give me but what this riband bound,
Take all the rest the sun goes round.

## " Go, Lovely Rose !"

GO, lovely Rose !
    Tell her that wastes her time and me,
That now she knows,
When I resemble her to thee,
How sweet and fair she seems to be.

    Tell her that's young,
And shuns to have her graces spied,
    That hadst thou sprung
In deserts, where no men abide,
Thou must have uncommended died.

    Small is the worth
Of beauty from the light retired ;
    Bid her come forth,
Suffer herself to be desired,
And not blush so to be admired.

    Then die ! that she
The common fate of all things rare
    May read in thee :
How small a part of time they share
That are so wondrous sweet and fair !

# Anonymous.

### HELEN OF KIRKCONNELL.

I WISH I were where Helen lies;
Night and day on me she cries;
O that I were where Helen lies,
    On fair Kirkconnell lee.

Curst be the heart that thought the thought,
And curst the hand that fired the shot,
When in my arms bird Helen dropt
    And died to succour me!

Oh, think ye na my heart was sair,
When my love dropt down and spake nae mair:
There did she swoon wi' meikle care,
    On fair Kirkconnell lee.

As I went down the water side,
None but my foe to be my guide,
None but my foe to be my guide
    On fair Kirkconnell lee—

I lighted down, my sword did draw,
I hacked him in pieces sma',

I hacked him in pieces sma'
　For her sake that died for me.

Oh, Helen, fair beyond compare!
I'll weave a garland of thy hair
Shall bind my heart for evermair,
　Until the day I dee.

Oh, that I were where Helen lies!
Night and day on me she cries;
Out of my bed she bids me rise,
　Says, " Haste and come to me!"

Oh, Helen fair!  Oh, Helen chaste!
Were I with thee I would be blest,
Where thou lies low and takes thy rest
　On fair Kirkconnell lee.

I wish my grave were growing green;
A winding sheet drawn o'er my e'en,
And I in Helen's arms lying
　On fair Kirkconnell lee.

I wish I were where Helen lies!
Night and day on me she cries,
And I am weary of the skies,
　For her sake that died for me.

## "Waly, Waly."

H, waly, waly up the bank,
    And waly, waly down the brae,
And waly, waly yon burn-side,
    Where I and my love wont to gae!
I leaned my bauk unto an aik,
    And thoucht it was a trusty tree;
But first it bowed and syne it brak:
    Sae my true-love did lichtlie me.

Oh, waly, waly, but love be bonnie
    A little time while it be new;
But when its auld it waxes cauld,
    And fades away like the morning dew.
Oh, wherefore should I busk my heid,
    Or wherefore should I kame my hair?
For my true-love has me forsook,
    And says he'll love me never mair.

Now Arthur's Seat shall be my bed,
    The sheets shall ne'er be pressed by me,
St. Anton's well shall be my drink,
    Since my true-love has forsaken me.
Martinmas wind, when wilt thou blaw,
    And shake the green leaves off the tree?

O gentle death, when wilt thou come?
  For of my life I am wearie.


'Tis not the fruit that freezes fell,
  Nor blawing men's inclemencie;
'Tis not sic cauld that makes me cry;
  But my love's heart's grown cauld to me.
When we came in by Glasgow toun,
  We were a comely sight to see;
My love was clad in the black velvet,
  And I mysel' in cramasie.


But had I wist before I kiss'd
  That love had been so ill to win,
I'd locked my heart in a case of gold,
  And pinn'd it wi' a siller pin.
Oh, oh, if my young babe was born,
  And set upon the nurse's knee,
And I mysel' were dead and gone,
  And the green grass growin' ower me!

# William Cartwright.

[Born 1611.    Died 1643.]

## To Cupid.

THOU who didst never see the light,
Nor know'st the pleasure of the sight,
But, always blinded, canst not say,
Now it is night, or now 'tis day ;
So captivate her sight, so blind her eye,
That still she love me, yet she ne'er know why.

Thou who dost wound us with such art,
We see no blood drop from the heart,
And, subt'ly cruel, leav'st no sign
To tell the blow or hand was thine ;
O gently, gently wound my fair, that she
May thence believe the wound did come from me.

# James, Marquis of Montrose.

[Born 1612.   Died 1650.]

---

## I'LL NEVER LOVE THEE MORE.

MY dear and only love, I pray
   That little world of thee
Be governed by no other sway
   But purest monarchy;
For if confusion have a part,
   Which virtuous souls abhor,
I'll call a synod in my heart,
   And never love thee more.

As Alexander I will reign,
   And I will reign alone;
My thoughts did evermore disdain
   A rival on my throne.
He either fears his fate too much
   Or his deserts are small,
Who dares not put it to the touch
   To gain or lose it all.

8*

But I will reign and govern still,
  And always give the law,
And have each subject at my will,
  And all to stand in awe;
But 'gainst my batteries if I find
  Thou storm or vex me sore,
As if thou set me as a blind,
  I'll never love thee more.

And in the empire of thy heart,
  Where I should solely be,
If others do pretend a part,
  Or dare to share with me;
Or committees if thou erect,
  Or go on such a score,
I'll smiling mock at thy neglect,
  And never love thee more.

But if no faithless action stain
  Thy love and constant word,
I'll make thee famous by my pen,
  And glorious by my sword;
I'll serve thee in such noble ways
  As ne'er was known before;
I'll deck and crown thy head with bays,
  And love thee evermore.

# Sir John Suckling.

[Born 1613.   Died 1641.]

## SONG.

ONEST lover, whosoever,
If in all thy love there ever
Was one wavering thought, if thy flame
Were not still even, still the same ;
  Know this,
    Thou lovest amiss,
      And to love true
Thou must begin again, and love anew.

If when she appears i' th' room,
Thou dost not quake, art not struck dumb ;
And if in striving this to cover
Dost not speak thy words twice over ;
  Know this,
    Thou lovest amiss,
      And to love true
Thou must begin again, and love anew.

If fondly thou dost not mistake,
And all defects for graces take,
Persuadest thyself that jests are broken,
When she has little or nothing spoken:
　　　Know this,
　　　　Thou lovest amiss,
　　　　　And to love true
Thou must begin again, and love anew.


If when thou appearest to be within,
Thou let'st not men ask, and ask again;
And when thou answerest, if it be
To what was asked thee properly:
　　　Know this,
　　　　Thou lovest amiss,
　　　　　And to love true
Thou must begin again, and love anew.


If when thy stomach calls to eat,
Thou cut'st not fingers 'stead of meat;
And with much gazing on her face,
Dost not rise hungry from the place:
　　　Know this,
　　　　Thou lovest amiss,
　　　　　And to love true
Thou must begin again, and love anew.

If by this thou dost discover
That thou art no perfect lover,
And desiring to love true
Thou dost begin to love anew :
    Know this,
      Thou lovest amiss,
        And to love true
Thou must begin again, and love anew.

# Richard Crashaw.

[Born 1615 (?).　Died 1652.]

## "THE DEW NO MORE SHALL WEEP."

THE dew no more shall weep,
　The primrose's pale cheek to deck ;
The dew no more shall sleep
　Nuzzled in the lily's neck :
Much rather would it tremble here,
And leave them both to be thy tear.

Not the soft gold which
　Steals from the amber-weeping tree,
Makes sorrow half so rich
　As the drops distilled from thee :
Sorrow's best jewels be in these
Caskets, of which Heaven keeps the keys.

When Sorrow would be seen
　In her bright majesty,
For she is a Queen,
　Then she is dressed by none but thee ;
Then, and only then, she wears
Her richest pearls ;—I mean thy tears.

Not in the evening's eyes,
   When they red with weeping are
For the sun that dies,
   Sits Sorrow with a face so fair :
Nowhere but here doth meet
Sweetness so sad, sadness so sweet.

---

Wishes for the supposed Mistress.

WHOE'ER  she be,
    That not impossible She
That shall command my heart and me !

    Where'er she lie,
    Locked up from mortal eye
In shady leaves of destiny ;

    Till that ripe birth
    Of studied Fate stand forth,
And teach her fair steps to our earth ;

    Till that divine
    Idea take a shrine
Of crystal flesh, through which to shine :

—Meet you her my Wishes,
Bespeak her to my blisses,
And be ye called, my absent kisses.

I wish her beauty
That owes not all its duty
To gaudy tire, or glistering shoe-tie :

Something more than
Taffeta or tissue can,
Or rampant feather, or rich fan.

A face that's best
By its own beauty drest,
And can alone command the rest :

A face made up
Out of no other shop
Than what Nature's white hand sets ope.

Sydneian showers
Of sweet discourse, whose powers
Can crown old Winter's head with flowers.

Whate'er delight
Can make day's forehead bright,
Or give down to the wings of night.

Soft, silken hours,
Open suns, shady bowers ;
'Bove all, nothing within that lowers.

Days, that need borrow
No part of their good-morrow
From a fore-spent night of sorrow :

Days, that in spite
Of darkness, by the light
Of a clear mind are day all night.

Life, that dares send
A challenge to his end,
And when it comes, says, " Welcome, friend."

I wish her store
Of worth may leave her poor
Of wishes ; and I wish—no more.

—Now if Time knows
That Her, whose radiant brows
Weave them a garland of my vows ;

Her that dares be
What these lines wish to see :
I seek no further, it is She.

'Tis She, and here,
Lo! I unclothe and clear
My wishes, cloudy character.

Such worth as this is
Shall fix my flying wishes,
And determine them to kisses.

Let her full glory,
My fancies, fly before ye;
Be ye my fictions:—but her story.

# Richard Lovelace.

[Born 1618.   Died 1658.]

## "Tell me not, Sweet."

TELL me not, sweet, I am unkind,
   That from the nunnery
Of thy chaste breast and quiet mind,
   To war and arms I fly.

True, a new mistress now I chase,
   The first foe in the field;
And with a stronger faith embrace
   A sword, a horse, a shield.

Yet this inconstancy is such,
   As you, too, shall adore;
I could not love thee, dear, so much,
   Loved I not honor more.

# Abraham Cowley.

[BORN 1618.  DIED 1667.]

## A SUPPLICATION.

AWAKE, awake, my Lyre!
  And tell thy silent master's humble tale
    In sounds that may prevail;
  Sounds that gentle thoughts inspire:
      Though so exalted she
      And I so lowly be,
Tell her, such different notes make all thy harmony.

      Hark! how the strings awake:
And though the moving hand approach not near,
    Themselves with awful fear
  A kind of numerous trembling make.
      Now all thy forces try;
      Now all thy charms apply;
Revenge upon her ear the conquests of her eye.

      Weak Lyre! thy virtue sure
Is useless here, since thou art only found

To cure, and not to wound,
And she to wound, but not to cure.
Too weak too wilt thou prove
My passion to remove ;
Physic to other ills, thou'rt nourishment to love.


Sleep, sleep again, my Lyre !
For thou canst never tell my humble tale
In sounds that will prevail,
Nor gentle thoughts in her inspire ;
All thy vain mirth lay by,
Bid thy strings silent lie,
Sleep, sleep again, my Lyre, and let thy master die.

---

## INCONSTANT.

HA! HA! you think you've killed my fame
By this not understood, yet common name ;
A name that's full and proper when assigned
To womankind ;
But when you call us so,
It can at best but for a metaphor go.


Can you the shore inconstant call,
Which still, as waves pass by, embraces all,

9*

That had as lief the same waves always love,
    Did they not from him move;
    Or can you fault with pilots find
For changing course, yet never blame the wind?


    Since drunk with vanity you fell,
The things turn round to you that steadfast dwell;
And you yourself who from us take your flight,
    Wonder to find us out of sight;
    So the same error seizes you,
As men in motion think the trees move too.

-------

### THE DISCOVERY.

BY Heaven, I'll tell her boldly that 'tis she;
  Why should she ashamed or angry be
    To be beloved by me?
    The gods may give their altars o'er,
    They'll smoke but seldom any more,
If none but happy men must them adore.


The lightning which tall oaks oppose in vain,
  To strike sometimes does not disdain
  The humble furzes of the plain.

She being so high, and I so low,
  Her power by this does greater show,
Who at such distance gives so sure a blow.

Compared with her all things so worthless prove,
    That naught on earth can to'ards her move,
    Till 't be exalted by her love.
    Equal to her, alas! there's none;
    She like a deity is grown,
That must create, or else must be alone.

If there be man who thinks himself so high
    As to pretend equality,
    He deserves her less than I;
    For he would cheat for his relief,
    And one would give with lesser grief
To an undeserving beggar than a thief.

# Alexander Brome.

[Born 1620. Died 1666.]

### THE RESOLVE.

TELL me not of a face that's fair,
  Nor lip and cheek that's red,
Nor of the tresses of her hair,
  Nor curls in order laid ;
Nor of a rare seraphic voice,
  That like an angel sings ;
Though, if I were to take my choice,
  I would have all these things.
But if that thou wilt have me love,
  And it must be a she ;
The only argument can move
  Is, that she will love me.

The glories of your ladies be
  But metaphors of things,
And but resemble what we see
  Each common object brings.
Roses outred their lips and cheeks,
  Lilies their whiteness stain :

What fool is he that shadow seeks,
  And may the substance gain?
Then, if thou'lt have me love a lass,
  Let it be one that's kind,
Else I'm a servant to the glass
  That's with canary lined.

# Andrew Marvel.

[Born 1620.　Died 1678.]

## The Picture of T. C. in a Prospect of Flowers.

SEE with what simplicity
　　This nymph begins her golden days!
In the green grass she loves to lie,
And there with her fair aspect tames
The wilder flowers, and gives them names;
　　But only with the roses plays,
　　　　And them does tell
What colour best becomes them, and what smell.

Who can foretell for what high cause
　　This darling of the gods was born?
See, this is she whose chaster laws
The wanton Love shall one day fear,
And, under her command severe,
　　See his bow broke and ensigns torn.
　　　　Happy who can
Appease this virtuous enemy of man!

O then let me in time compound,
　And parley with those conquering eyes ;
Ere they have tried their force to wound,
Ere with their glancing wheels they drive
In triumph over hearts that strive,
　And them that yield but more despise,
　　Let me be laid
Where I may see the glory from some shade.


　Meanwhile, whilst every verdant thing
　　Itself does at thy beauty charm,
Reform the errors of the spring ;
Make that the tulips may have share
Of sweetness, seeing they are fair ;
　And roses of their thorns disarm :
　　But most procure
That violets may a longer age endure.


But oh, young beauty of the woods,
　Whom nature courts with fruit and flowers,
Gather the flowers, but spare the buds ;
Lest Flora, angry at thy crime
To kill her infants in their prime,
　Should quickly make the example yours ;
　　And, ere we see,
Nip in the blossom all our hopes in thee.

# John Dryden.

[BORN 1631.   DIED 1701.]

---

### "AH! HOW SWEET!"

AH! how sweet it is to love!
    Ah! how gay is young desire;
And what pleasing pains we prove,
    When we first approach love's fire:—
Pains of love are sweeter far
Than all other pleasures are.*

Sighs which are from lovers blown
    Do but gently heave the heart:
E'en the tears they shed alone,
    Cure, like trickling balm, their smart.
Lovers, when they lose their breath,
Bleed away in easy death.

Love and Time with reverence use,
    Treat them like a parting friend;

---

* Burns has used this idea in one of his songs.   He shapes it thus:

    " 'Twere better for thee despairing,
      Than aught in the world beside, Jessie."

Nor the golden gifts refuse
  Which in youth sincere they send :
For each year their price is more,
And they less simple than before.

Love, like spring-tides full and high,
  Swells in every youthful vein ;
But each tide does less supply,
  Till they quite shrink in again.
If a flow in age appear,
'Tis but rain, and runs not clear.

----

## " FAIR, SWEET, AND YOUNG."

FAIR, sweet, and young, receive a prize
  Reserved for your victorious eyes ;
From crowds, whom at your feet you see,
O pity and distinguish me !
As I, from thousand beauties more
Distinguish you, and only you adore.

Your face for conquest was designed ;
Your every motion charms my mind ;

Angels, when you your silence break,
Forget their hymns to hear you speak ;
But when at once they hear and view,
Are loth to mount, and long to stay with you.

No graces can your form improve,
But all are lost unless you love ;
While that sweet passion you disdain,
Your veil and beauty are in vain :
In pity then prevent my fate,
For after dying, all reprieve's too late.

# Sir George Etherege.

[Born 1636(?).   Died 1683.]

---

## "Cease, anxious World."

CEASE, anxious world, your fruitless pain,
  To grasp forbidden store ;
Your sturdy labors shall prove vain,
  Your alchemy unblest ;
Whilst seeds of far more precious ore
  Are ripened in my breast.

My breast the forge of happier love,
  Where my Lucinda lives ;
And the rich stock does so improve,
  As she her art employs,
That every smile and touch she gives
  Turns all to golden joys.

Since then we can such treasures raise,
  Let's no expense refuse ;
In love let's lay out all our days ;
  How can we e'er be poor,
When every blessing that we use
  Begets a thousand more ?

# Charles Sackville, Earl of Dorset.

[Born 1637.   Died 1706.]

### "To all you Ladies."

TO all you ladies now on land,
　　We men at sea indite;
But first would have you understand
　　How hard it is to write;
The Muses now, and Neptune too,
We must implore to write to you,
　　With a fa, la, la, la, la.

For though the Muses should prove kind,
　　And fill our empty brain;
Yet if rough Neptune rouse the wind,
　　To wave the azure main,
Our paper, pen and ink, and we,
Roll up and down in ships at sea,
　　With a fa, la, la, la, la.

Then if we write not by each post,
　　Think not we are unkind;
Nor yet conclude our ships are lost
　　By Dutchmen or by wind:

Our tears we'll send a speedier way—
The tide shall bring them twice a day.
   With a fa, la, la, la, la.

The king, with wonder and surprise,
   Will swear the seas grow bold;
Because the tides will higher rise
   Than e'er they did of old;
But let him know it is our tears
Bring floods of grief to Whitehall stairs.
   With a fa, la, la, la, la.

Should foggy Opdam chance to know
   Our sad and dismal story,
The Dutch would scorn so weak a foe,
   And quit their fort at Goree:
For what resistance can they find
From men who've left their hearts behind?
   With a fa, la, la, la, la.

Let wind and weather do its worst,
   Be ye to us but kind;
Let Dutchmen vapor, Spaniards curse,
   No sorrow shall we find;
'Tis then no matter how things go,
Or who's our friend, or who's our foe.
   With a fa, la, la, la, la.

To pass our tedious hours away,
   We throw a merry main,
Or else at serious ombre play;
   But why should we in vain
Each other's ruin thus pursue?
We were undone when we left you.
    With a fa, la, la, la, la.


But now our fears tempestuous grow,
   And cast our hopes away;
Whilst you, regardless of our woe,
   Sit careless at a play:
Perhaps permit some happier man
To kiss your hand or flirt your fan.
    With a fa, la, la, la, la.


When any mournful tune you hear
   That dies in every note,
As if it sighed with each man's care
   For being so remote;
Then think how often love we've made
To you, when all those tunes were played.
    With a fa, la, la, la, la.


In justice you cannot refuse
   To think of our distress,

When we for hopes of honors lose
   Our certain happiness :
All those designs are but to prove
Ourselves more worthy of your love.
   With a fa, la, la, la, la.


And now we've told you all our loves,
   And likewise all our fears ;
In hopes this declaration moves
   Some pity for our tears ;
Let's hear of no inconstancy,
We have too much of that at sea.
   With a fa, la, la, la, la.

# Sir Charles Sedley.

[Born 1639.   Died 1701.]

---

### Child and Maiden.

AH, Chloris! could I now but sit
  As unconcerned as when
Your infant beauty could beget
  No happiness or pain!
When I the dawn used to admire,
  And praised the coming day,
I little thought the rising fire
  Would take my rest away.


Your charms in harmless childhood lay
  Like metals in a mine ;
Age from no face takes more away
  Than youth concealed in thine.
But as your charms insensibly
  To their perfection prest,
So love as unperceived did fly,
  And centered in my breast.

My passion with your beauty grew,
  While Cupid at my heart,
Still, as his mother favoured you,
  Threw a new flaming dart :
Each gloried in their wanton part ;
  To make a lover, he
Employed the utmost of his art—
  To make a beauty, she.

# Thomas Stanley.

[Born 1644.   Died 1678.]

### THE DEPOSITION.

THOUGH when I loved thee thou wert fair,
　　Thou art no longer so :
Those glories, all the pride they wear
　　Unto opinion owe :
Beauties, like stars, in borrowed lustre shine,
And 'twas my love that gave thee thine.

The flames that dwelt within thine eye
　　Do now with mine expire ;
Thy brightest graces fade and die
　　At once with my desire.
Love's fires thus mutual influence return ;
Thine cease to shine when mine to burn.

Then, proud Celinda, hope no more
　　To be implored or wooed ;
Since by thy scorn thou dost restore
　　The wealth my love bestowed ;
And thy despised disdain too late shall find
That none are fair but who are kind.

# John Wilmot, Earl of Rochester.

[Born 1647.   Died 1680.]

### Song.

HILE on these lovely looks I gaze,
　To see a wretch pursuing,
In raptures of a blest amaze,
　His pleasing, happy ruin;
'Tis not for pity that I move;
　His fate is too aspiring,
Whose heart, broke with a load of love,
　Dies wishing and admiring.

But if this murder you'd forego,
　Your slave from death removing,
Let me your art of charming know,
　Or learn you mine of loving.
But whether life or death betide,
　In love 'tis equal measure;
The victor lives with empty pride,
　The vanquished die with pleasure.

# Francis Atterbury, Bp. of Rochester.

[Born 1662.   Died 1732.]

## THE LOVER'S VOW.

FAIR  Sylvia, cease to blame my youth
  For having loved before;
For men, till they have learned the truth,
  Strange deities adore.

My heart, 'tis true, hath often ranged,
  Like bees on gaudy flowers;
And many a thousand loves hath changed,
  Till it was fixed on yours.

But, Sylvia, when I saw those eyes,
  'Twas soon determined there;
Stars might as well forsake the skies,
  And vanish into air.

When I from this great rule do err,
  New beauties to adore,
May I again turn wanderer,
  And never settle more.

# William Walsh.

[Born 1663. Died 1709.]

---

### Rivalry in Love.

F all the torments, all the cares,
   With which our lives are curst;
Of all the plagues a lover bears,
   Sure rivals are the worst!
By partners of each other kind,
   Affections easier grow;
In love alone we hate to find
   Companions of our woe.

Sylvia, for all the pangs you see
   Are labouring in my breast,
I beg not you would favour me,
   Would you but slight the rest
How great soe'er your rigors are,
   With them alone I'll cope;
I can endure my own despair,
   But not another's hope.

# Matthew Prior.

[BORN 1664.　DIED 1721.]

SONG.

THE merchant, to secure his treasure,
　　Conveys it in a borrowed name;
Euphelia serves to grace my measure,
　　But Cloe is my real flame.

My softest verse, my darling lyre
　　Upon Euphelia's toilet lay—
When Cloe noted her desire
　　That I should sing, that I should play.

My lyre I tune, my voice I raise,
　　But with my numbers mix my sighs;
And whilst I sing Euphelia's praise,
　　I fix my soul on Cloe's eyes.

Fair Cloe blushed: Euphelia frowned;
　　I sung and gazed; I played and trembled;
And Venus to the Loves around
　　Remarked how ill we all dissembled.

# Aaron Hill.

[Born 1684-5.  Died 1749-50.]

## MODESTY.

AS lamps burn silent with unconscious light,
So modest ease in beauty shines most bright:
Unaiming charms with edge resistless fall,
And she who means no mischief does it all.

## SONG.

H! forbear to bid me slight her,
    Soul and senses take her part;
Could my death itself delight her,
    Life should leap to leave my heart.
Strong, though soft, a lover's chain,
Charmed with woe, and pleased with pain.

Though the tender flame were dying,
    Love would light it at her eyes;
Or, her tuneful voice applying,
    Through my ear my soul surprise.
Deaf, I see the fate I shun;
Blind, I fear I am undone.

# James Thomson.

[BORN 1700.    DIED 1748.]

## SONG.

FOREVER, Fortune, wilt thou prove
An unrelenting foe to Love,
And when we meet a mutual heart,
Come in between and bid us part?

Bid us sigh on from day to day,
And wish and wish the soul away;
Till youth and genial years are flown,
And all the life of life is gone?

But busy, busy still art thou,
To bind the loveless, joyless vow,
The heart from pleasure to delude,
To join the gentle to the rude.

For once, O Fortune, hear my prayer,
And I absolve thy future care;
All other blessings I resign,
Make but the dear Amanda mine.

# David Mallet.

[Born 1700 (?).  Died 1765.]

SONG.

THE smiling morn, the breathing spring,
Invite the tuneful birds to sing:
And while they warble from each spray,
Love melts the universal lay.
Let us, Amanda, timely wise,
Like them improve the hour that flies;
And, in soft raptures, waste the day,
Among the shades of Endermay.

Too soon the winter of the year,
And age, life's winter, will appear:
At this, thy living bloom must fade;
As that will strip the verdant shade.
Our taste of pleasure then is o'er;
The feathered songsters love no more:
And when they droop and we decay,
Adieu the shades of Endermay.

11*

# William Pattison.

[Born 1706.    Died 1727.]

### To her Ring.

BLEST ornament! how happy is thy snare,
To bind the snowy finger of my fair!
   O could I learn thy nice coercive art,
   And, as thou bind'st her fingers, bind her
     heart!

Not eastern diadems like thee can shine,
Fed from her brighter eyes with beams divine;
Nor can their mightiest monarch's power command
So large an empire as thy charmer's hand.

O could thy form thy fond admirer wear,
Thy very likeness should in all appear;
My endless love thy endless round should show,
And my heart flaming, for thy diamond glow.

# George, Lord Lyttelton.

[BORN 1709. DIED 1773.]

### "TELL ME, MY HEART."

WHEN Delia on the plain appears,
Awed by a thousand tender fears,
I would approach, but dare not move;
Tell me, my heart, if this be love?

Whene'er she speaks, my ravished ear
No other voice than hers can hear,
No other wit but hers approve;
Tell me, my heart, if this be love?

If she some other swain commend,
Though I was once his fondest friend,
His instant enemy I prove;—
Tell me, my heart, if this be love?

When she is absent, I no more
Delight in all that pleased before,
The clearest spring, the shadiest grove;
Tell me, my heart, if this be love?

When, fond of power, of beauty vain,
Her nets she spreads for every swain,
I strove to hate, but vainly strove;—
Tell me, my heart, if this be love?

# Tobias Smollett, M. D.

[BORN 1720.   DIED 1774.]

### SONG.

O fix her—'twere a task as vain
To count the April drops of rain,
To sow in Afric's barren soil,
Or tempests hold within a toil.

I know it, friend, she's light as air,
False as the fowler's artful snare;
Inconstant as the passing wind,
As winter's dreary frost unkind.

She's such a miser too in love,
Its joys she'll neither share nor prove;
Though hundreds of gallants await
From her victorious eyes their fate.

Blushing at such inglorious reign,
I sometimes strive to break her chain;
My reason summon to my aid,
Resolved no more to be betrayed.

Ah! friend, 'tis but a short-lived trance,
Dispelled by one enchanting glance;
She need but look, and I confess,
Those looks completely curse or bless.

So soft, so elegant, so fair,
Sure something more than human's there;
I must submit, for strife is vain,
'Twas destiny that forged the chain.

# Mark Akenside, M. D.

[Born 1721.  Died 1770.]

### "THE SHAPE ALONE."*

THE shape alone let others prize,
  The features of the fair;
I look for spirit in her eyes,
  And meaning in her air.

A damask cheek and ivory arm
  Shall ne'er my wishes win;
Give me an animated form
  That speaks a mind within;

A face where awful honor shines,
  Where sense and sweetness move,
And angel innocence refines
  The tenderness of love.

These are the soul of beauty's frame,
  Without whose vital aid

* There is some doubt about the authorship of this.  It is attributed to Akenside, but is not to be found in his collected poems.

Unfinished all her features seem,
    And all her roses dead.

But, ah ! where both their charms unite,
    How perfect is the view,
With every image of delight,
    With graces ever new !

Of power to charm the deepest woe,
    The wildest rage control ;
Diffusing mildness o'er the brow
    And rapture through the soul.

Their power but faintly to express
    All language must despair ;
But go behold Aspasia's face,
    And read it perfect there.

# Thomas Percy, Bishop of Dromore.

[BORN 1728.   DIED 1811.]

"O NANCY, WILT THOU GO WITH ME."

NANCY! wilt thou go with me,
  Nor sigh to leave this flaunting town?
Can silent glens have charms for thee,
  The lowly cot and russet gown?
No longer drest in silken sheen,
  No longer deck'd with jewels rare,
Say, canst thou quit each courtly scene
  Where thou wert fairest of the fair?

O Nancy! when thou'rt far away,
  Wilt thou not cast a wish behind?
Say, canst thou face the parching ray,
  Nor shrink before the wintry wind?
O can that soft and gentle mien
  Extremes of hardship learn to bear,
Nor sad regret each courtly scene
  Where thou wert fairest of the fair?

12

O Nancy ! canst thou love so true,
 Through perils keen with me to go,
Or when thy swain mishap shall rue,
 To share with him the pang of woe ?
Say, should disease or pain befall,
 Wilt thou assume the nurse's care,
Nor wistful those gay scenes recall
 Where thou wert fairest of the fair ?

And when at last thy love shall die,
 Wilt thou receive his parting breath ?
Wilt thou repress each struggling sigh,
 And cheer with smiles the bed of death ?
And wilt thou o'er his breathless clay
 Strew flowers, and drop the tender tear,
Nor then regret those scenes so gay
 Where thou wert fairest of the fair ? *

---

* There is a Scotch variation of this poem, differing only in substi
tuting " Nannie" for " Nancy," and " gang" for " go."  We give th.
lines as originally published.

# William Julius Mickle.

[Born 1734.  Died 1788.]

---

## "There's nae Luck about the House."

BUT are ye sure the news is true?
  And are ye sure he's weel?
Is this a time to think o' wark?
  Ye jauds, fling bye your wheel!
    For there's nae luck about the house,
      There's nae luck at a';
    There's nae luck about the house
      When our gudeman's awa.

Is this a time to think o' wark,
  When Colin's at the door?
Rax doun my cloak—I'll to the quay,
  And see him come ashore.

Rise up and mak a clean fireside,
  Put on the muckle pot;
Gie little Kate her cotton goun,
  And Jock his Sunday's coat.

And mak their shoon as black as slaes,
　　Their stockins white as snaw ;
It's a' to pleasure our gudeman—
　　He likes to see them braw.

There are twa hens into the crib
　　Hae fed this month or mair ;
Mak haste and thraw their necks about,
　　That Colin weel may fare.

My Turkey slippers I'll put on,
　　My stockins o' pearl blue—
It's a' to pleasure our gudeman,
　　For he's baith leal and true.

Sae sweet his voice, sae smooth his tongue,
　　His breath's like caller air ;
His very foot has music in't,
　　As he comes up the stair.

And will I see his face again,
　　And will I hear him speak ?
I'm dounricht dizzy with the thocht,
　　In troth I'm like to greet.

There's nae luck about the house,
　　There's nae luck at a' ;
There's nae luck about the house
　　When our gudeman's awa.

# Graham (of Cartmore).

[BORN 1735. DIED 1797.]

"TELL ME HOW TO WOO THEE."

IF doughty deeds my lady please,
  Right soon I'll mount my steed;
And strong his arm and fast his seat
  That bears frae me the meed.
I'll wear thy colours in my cap,
  Thy picture at my heart;
And he that bends not to thine eye
  Shall rue it to his smart!
Then tell me how to woo thee, Love,
  O tell me how to woo thee!
For thy dear sake, nae care I'll take,
  Though ne'er another trow me.

If gay attire delight thine eye,
  I'll dight me in array;
I'll tend thy chamber door all night,
  And squire thee all the day.

12*

If sweetest sounds can win thine ear,
   These sounds I'll strive to catch;
Thy voice I'll steal to woo thysel,
   That voice that none can match.

But if fond love thy heart can gain,
   I never broke a vow;
Nae maiden lays her skaith to me,
   I never loved but you.
For you alone I ride the ring,
   For you I wear the blue;
For you alone I strive to sing,
   O tell me how to woo!
Then tell me how to woo thee, Love;
   O tell me how to woo thee!
For thy dear sake, nae care I'll take,
   Though ne'er another trow me.

# Anne Hunter.

[Born 1742.  Died 1821.]

---

## "MY MOTHER BIDS ME BIND MY HAIR."

Y mother bids me bind my hair
  With bands of rosy hue,
Tie up my sleeves with ribands rare,
  And lace my bodice blue :
For why, she cries, sit still and weep,
  While others dance and play?
Alas! I scarce can go or creep
  While Lubin is away.

'Tis sad to think the days are gone
  When those we love are near :
I sit upon this mossy stone,
  And sigh when none can hear.
And while I spin my flaxen thread,
  And sing my simple lay,
The village seems asleep, or dead,
  While Lubin is away.

# Charles Dibdin.

[Born 1745.   Died 1814]

### Song.

IF 'tis love to wish you near,
To tremble when the wind I hear,
   Because at sea you floating rove ;
If of you to dream at night,
To languish when you're out of sight,—
   If this be loving, then I love.

If when you're gone, to count each hour,
To ask of every tender power
   That you may kind and faithful prove ;
If, void of falsehood and deceit,
I feel a pleasure now we meet,—
   If this be loving, then I love.

To wish your fortune to partake,
Determined never to forsake,
   Though low in poverty we strove ;
If, so that me your wife you'd call,
I offer you my little all,—
   If this be loving, then I love.

# John Lapraik.

[Born 1746(?). Died 1807.]

### MATRIMONIAL HAPPINESS.*

WHEN I upon thy bosom lean,
    And fondly clasp thee a' my ain,
I glory in the sacred ties
    That made us ane wha ance were twain.
A mutual flame inspires us baith,
    The tender look, the meltin' kiss ;
Even years shall ne'er destroy our love,
    But only gie us change o' bliss.

Hae I a wish ? it's a' for thee !
    I ken thy wish is me to please ;
Our moments pass sae smooth away,
    That numbers on us look and gaze ;
Weel pleased they see our happy days,
    Nor envy's sel' finds aught to blame ;

* An Anglicised version of the above lines was published by George
Huddesford ; and this, from a copy having been found among the papers
of Lindley Murray, after his death, was generally attributed to the latter.

And aye when weary cares arise,
  Thy bosom still shall be my hame.

I'll lay me there and tak' my rest ;
  And if that aught disturb my dear,
I'll bid her laugh her cares away,
  And beg her not to drop a tear.
Hae I a joy ? it's a' her ain !
  United still her heart and mine ;
They're like the woodbine round the tree,
  That's twined till death shall them disjoin.

# Hector M'Neill.

[Born 1746.  Died 1818.]

### My Boy Tammy.

WHAR hae ye been a' day,
  My boy Tammy?
I've been by burn and flow'ry brae,
Meadow green and mountain grey,
Courting o' this young thing,
  Just come frae her mammy.

And whar gat ye that young thing,
  My boy Tammy?
I got her doun in yonder howe,
Smiling on a bonny knowe,
Herding ae wee lamb and ewe
  For her poor mammy.

What said ye to the bonnie bairn,
  My boy Tammy?
I praised her e'en sae lovely blue,
Her dimpled cheek and cherry mou',
I preed it aft, as ye may trow,—
  She said she'd tell her mammy.

I held her to my beating heart
  My young, my smiling lammie;
I hae a house, it cost me dear,
I've walth o' plenishin and gear;
Ye'se get it a', wer't ten times mair,
  Gin ye will leave your mammy.

The smile gaed aff her bonny face—
  I maunna leave my mammy;
She's gien me meat, she's gien me claise,
She's been my comfort a' my days!
My father's death brought many waes;
  I canna leave my mammy.

We'll tak' her hame and mak' her fain,
  My ain kind-hearted lammie;
We'll gie her meat, we'll gie her claise,
We'll be her comfort a' her days.
The wee thing gies her hand and says,
  There, gang and ask my mammy.

Has she been to the kirk wi' thee,
  My boy Tammy?
She has been to the kirk wi' me,
And the tear was in her ee;
For, oh, she's but a young thing,
  Just come frae her mammy.

# Susanna Blamire.

[BORN 1747.   DIED 1794]

## THE WAEFU' HEART.*

GIN livin' worth could win my heart,
  You would not speak in vain ;
But in the darksome grave it's laid,
  Never to rise again.
My waefu' heart lies low with his,
  Whose heart was only mine ;
And, oh, what a heart was that to lose !
  But I maun not repine.

Yet, oh, gin Heaven in mercy soon
  Would grant the boon I crave,
And take this life, now naething worth,
  Sin' Jamie's in his grave !
And see, his gentle spirit comes,
  To shew me on my way ;
Surprised, nae doubt, I still am here,
  Sair wondering at my stay.

---

* Erroneously attributed, in the "Garland of Scotia," to Jeanie Ferguson.

13

I come, I come, my Jamie dear,
    And, oh, wi' what gudewill
I follow wheresoe'er ye lead !
    Ye canna lead to ill :—
She said, and soon a deadly pale
    Her faded cheek possess'd ;
Her waefu' heart forgot to beat,
    Her sorrows sunk to rest.

# Rev. John Logan.

[Born 1748.   Died 1788.]

### The Braes of Yarrow.

THY braes were bonnie, Yarrow stream,
    When first on them I met my lover;
Thy braes how dreary, Yarrow stream,
    When now thy waves his body cover!
Forever now, O Yarrow stream!
    Thou art to me a stream of sorrow;
For never on thy banks shall I
    Behold my love, the Flower of Yarrow!

He promised me a milk-white steed,
    To bear me to his father's bowers;
He promised me a little page,
    To squire me to his father's towers;
He promised me a wedding-ring—
    The wedding-day was fixed to-morrow:
Now he is wedded to his grave,
    Alas, his watery grave in Yarrow!

Sweet were his words when last we met ;
  My passion I as freely told him :
Clasped in his arms, I little thought
  That I should never more behold him.
Scarce was he gone, I saw his ghost ;
  It vanished with a shriek of sorrow :
Thrice did the water-wraith ascend,
  And gave a doleful groan through Yarrow.

His mother from the window looked,
  With all the longing of a mother ;
His little sister weeping walked
  The greenwood path to meet her brother ;
They sought him east, they sought him west,
  They sought him all the forest thorough ;
They only saw the cloud of night,
  They only heard the roar of Yarrow.

No longer from thy window look ;
  Thou hast no son, thou tender mother !
No longer walk, thou lovely maid ;
  Alas, thou hast no more a brother !
No longer seek him east or west,
  No longer search the forest thorough ;
For wandering in the night so dark,
  He fell a lifeless corpse in Yarrow.

The tear shall never leave my cheek,
  No other youth shall be my marrow ;
I'll seek thy body in the stream,
  And then with thee I'll sleep in Yarrow.
The tear did never leave her cheek,
  No other youth became her marrow ;
She found his body in the stream,
  And now with him she sleeps in Yarrow.

13*

# R. B. Sheridan.

[Born 1751.  Died 1816.]

## SONG.

HAD I a heart for falsehood framed,
  I ne'er could injure you ;
For though your tongue no promise claimed,
  Your charms would make me true :
To you no soul shall bear deceit,
  No stranger offer wrong,
But friends in all the aged you'll meet,
  And lovers in the young.


But when they learn that you have blest
  Another with your heart,
They'll bid aspiring passion rest,
  And act a brother's part ;
Then, lady, dread not here deceit,
  Nor fear to suffer wrong,
For friends in all the aged you'll meet,
  And lovers in the young.

# Thomas Chatterton.

[BORN 1752.   DIED 1770.]

MINSTREL'S SONG.

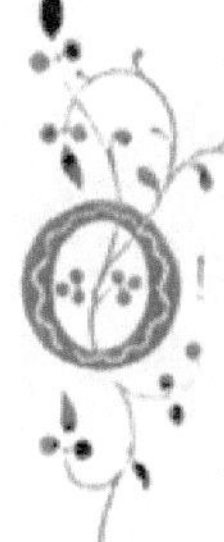

O! SING unto my roundelay,
    O! drop the briny tear with me;
Dance no more at holiday,
    Like a running river be;
        My love is dead,
        Gone to his death-bed,
    All under the willow-tree.

Black his hair as the winter night,
    White his skin as the driven snow,
Ruddy his face as the morning light,
    Cold he lies in the grave below;
        My love is dead,
        Gone to his death-bed,
    All under the willow-tree.

Sweet his tongue as the throstle's note,
    Quick in dance as thought could be,

Deft his tabour, cudgel stout ;
  O ! he lies by the willow-tree ;
    My love is dead,
      Gone to his death-bed,
  All under the willow-tree.


Hark ! the raven flaps his wing
  In the briered dell below ;
Hark ! the death-owl loud doth sing
  To the night-mares as they go ;
    My love is dead,
      Gone to his death-bed,
  All under the willow-tree.


See, the white moon shines on high ;
  Whiter is my true love's shroud ;
Whiter than the morning sky,
  Whiter than the evening cloud ;
    My love is dead,
      Gone to his death-bed,
  All under the willow-tree.


Here, upon my true love's grave,
  Shall the barren flowers be laid,
Not on holy saint to save
  All the celness of a maid ;

My love is dead,
Gone to his death-bed,
All under the willow-tree.

With my hands I'll dent the briers,
Round his holy corse to gre ;
Elves and fairies, light your fires,
Here my body still shall be ;
My love is dead,
Gone to his death-bed,
All under the willow-tree.

Come with acorn cup and thorn,
Drain my heart its blood away ;
Life and all its goods I scorn,
Dance by night or feast by day ;
My love is dead,
Gone to his death-bed,
All under the willow-tree.

# Robert Burns.

[Born 1759.    Died 1796.]

### John Anderson, my Jo.*

JOHN Anderson, my jo, John,
    When we were first acquent,
Your locks were like the raven,
    Your bonnie brow was brent;
But now your brow is bald, John,
    Your locks are like the snaw;
But blessings on your frosty pow,
    John Anderson, my jo.

John Anderson, my jo, John,
    They say 'tis forty year
Syne I ca'd you my jo, John,
    And you ca'd me your dear;
But there they're surely wrang, John;
    'Tis nae sae lang ago;

---

* The second stanza of the above is by some unknown writer.   Many
attempts at additional words have been made; but the above is the only
one in which the language and sentiment are at all equal to those in the
verses of Burns.

'Tis but a hinney-moon at maist,
John Anderson, my jo.

John Anderson, my jo, John,
  We clamb the hill thegither;
And mony a canty day, John,
  We've had wi' ane anither;
Now we maun totter down, John,
  But hand in hand we'll go,
And sleep thegither at the foot,
  John Anderson, my jo.

---

### FARE THEE WEEL.

AE fond kiss, and then we sever;
Ae fareweel, alas, for ever!
Deep in heart-wrung tears I'll pledge thee,
Warring sighs and groans I'll wage thee.
Who shall say that fortune grieves him
While the star of hope she leaves him?
Me nae cheerfu' twinkle lights me;
Dark despair around benights me.

I'll ne'er blame my partial fancy,
Naething could resist my Nancy;
But to see her was to love her,
Love but her, and love for ever.

Had we never loved sae kindly,
Had we never loved sae blindly,
Never met—or never parted,
We had ne'er been broken-hearted.

Fare thee weel, thou first and fairest ;
Fare thee weel, thou best and dearest ;
Thine be ilka joy and treasure,
Peace, enjoyment, love, and pleasure.
Ae fond kiss, and then we sever ;
Ae fareweel, alas, for ever !
Deep in heart-wrung tears I pledge thee,
Warring sighs and groans I'll wage thee.

-------

## HIGHLAND MARY.

YE banks and braes, and streams around
 The castle o' Montgomery,
Green be your woods and fair your flowers,
 Your waters never drumlie.
There Simmer first unfauld her robes,
 And there they langest tarry ;
For there I took the last fareweel
 O' my sweet Highland Mary.

How sweetly bloomed the gay green birk,
  How rich the hawthorn's blossom,
As underneath their fragrant shade
  I clasped her to my bosom!
The golden hours on angel wings
  Flew o'er me and my dearie;
For dear to me as light and life
  Was my sweet Highland Mary.

Wi' mony a vow and locked embrace,
  Our parting was fu' tender;
And pledging aft to meet again,
  We tore oursels asunder;
But, oh, fell death's untimely frost,
  That nipt my flower sae early;
Now green's the sod and cauld's the clay
  That wraps my Highland Mary!

Oh, pale, pale now those rosy lips
  I aft hae kissed sae fondly;
And closed for aye the sparkling glance
  That dwelt on me sae kindly;
And mould'ring now in silent dust
  That heart that lo'ed me dearly;
But still within my bosom's core
  Shall live my Highland Mary.

## "Of a' the Airts."

F a' the airts the wind can blaw
   I dearly like the west,
For there the bonnie lassie lives,
   The lassie I lo'e best:
There wild woods grow, and rivers row,
   And mony a hill between;
But day and night my fancy's flight
   Is ever wi' my Jean.

I see her in the dewy flowers,
   I see her sweet and fair;
I hear her in the tunefu' birds,
   I hear her charm the air:
There's not a bonnie flower that springs
   By fountain, shaw, or green,
There's not a bonnie bird that sings,
   But minds me o' my Jean.

## The Banks o' Doon.

YE banks and braes o' bonnie Doon,
  How can ye bloom sae fresh and fair?
How can ye chaunt, ye little birds,
  And I sae weary fou o' care!
Ye'll break my heart, ye little birds,
  That wanton through the flowery thorn;
Ye mind me o' departed joys,
  Departed never to return.

Aft hae I roved by bonnie Doon,
  To see the rose and woodbine twine;
Where ilka bird sang o' its luve,
  And fondly sae did I o' mine.
Wi' heartsome glee I pu'd a rose,
  The sweetest on its thorny tree;
But my fause love has stown the rose,
  And left the thorn behind wi' me.

# Thomas Russell.

[Born 1762.    Died 1788.]

## To Delia.

'TIS not a cheek that boasts the ruby's glow,
The neck of ivory or the breast of snow;
'Tis not a dimple known so oft to charm,
The hand's soft polish, or the tapering arm;
'Tis not the braided lock of golden hue,
Nor reddening lip that swells with vernal dew;
'Tis not a smile that blooms with young desire;
'Tis not an eye that sheds celestial fire;
No, Delia! these are not the spells that move
My heart to fold thee in eternal love:
But 'tis that Soul, which from so fair a frame
Looks truth, and tells us—'twas from Heaven it
    came!

# Samuel Rogers.

[Born 1762.   Died 1855.]

### The Sleeping Beauty.

SLEEP on, and dream of Heaven awhile—
    Though shut so close thy laughing eyes,
Thy rosy lips still wear a smile,
    And move, and breathe delicious sighs.

Ah, now soft blushes tinge her cheeks
    And mantle o'er her neck of snow ;
Ah, now she murmurs, now she speaks,
    What most I wish—and fear to know !

She starts, she trembles, and she weeps !
    Her fair hands folded on her breast :
—And now, how like a saint she sleeps !
    A seraph in the realms of rest !

Sleep on secure !   Above control,
    Thy thoughts belong to Heaven and thee ;
And may the secret of thy soul
    Remain within its sanctuary !

14*

# William Wordsworth.

[Born 1770. Died 1850.]

---

### A Picture.

SHE was a phantom of delight
When first she gleamed upon my sight ;
A lovely apparition, sent
To be a moment's ornament ;
Her eyes as stars of twilight fair ;
Like Twilight's, too, her dusky hair ;
But all things else about her, drawn
From May-time and the cheerful dawn ;
A dancing shape, an image gay,
To haunt, to startle, and waylay.

I saw her upon nearer view,
A spirit, yet a woman too !
Her household motions light and free,
And steps of virgin-liberty ;
A countenance in which did meet
Sweet records, promises as sweet ;
A creature not too bright or good
For human nature's daily food,

For transient sorrows, simple wiles,
Praise, blame, love, kisses, tears, and smiles.

And now I see with eye serene
The very pulse of the machine ;
A being breathing thoughtful breath,
A traveller between life and death :
The reason firm, the temperate will,
Endurance, foresight, strength, and skill ;
A perfect woman, nobly planned,
To warn, to comfort, and command,
And yet a Spirit still, and bright
With something of an angel-light.

## THE LOST LOVE.

HE dwelt among the untrodden ways
    Beside the springs of Dove ;
A maid whom there were none to praise,
    And very few to love.

A violet by a mossy stone
    Half hidden from the eye !
—Fair as a star, when only one
    Is shining in the sky.

She lived unknown, and few could know
   When Lucy ceased to be ;
But she is in her grave, and O !
   The difference to me.

---

### THE DEAD LOVE.

A SLUMBER did my spirit seal ;
   I had no human fears :
She seemed a thing that could not feel
   The touch of early years.

No motion has she now, nor force ;
   She neither hears nor sees ;
Rolled round in earth's diurnal course
   With rocks, and stones, and trees.

# Sir Walter Scott.

[BORN 1771.   DIED 1832.]

## "A Weary Lot is Thine."

WEARY lot is thine, fair maid,
  A weary lot is thine;
To pull the thorn thy brow to braid,
  And press the rue for wine.
A lightsome eye, a soldier's mien,
  A feather of the blue,
A doublet of the Lincoln green,—
No more of me you knew, my love,
  No more of me you knew.

This morn is merry June, I trow,
  The rose is budding fain;
But it shall bloom in winter snow
  Ere we two meet again.
He turned his charger as he spoke
  Upon the river-shore;
He gave his bridle reins a shake,
Said, Adieu for evermore, my love,
  And adieu for evermore!

## SONG.

WHERE shall the lover rest
    Whom the fates sever
From his true maiden's breast,
    Parted for ever?
Where, through groves deep and high,
    Sounds the far billow,
Where early violets die
    Under the willow.
        Eleu loro
    Soft shall be his pillow.

There, through the summer day,
    Cool streams are laving:
There, while the tempests sway,
    Scarce are boughs waving;
There thy rest shalt thou take,
    Parted for ever,
Never again to wake,
    Never, O never!
        Eleu loro
    Never, O never!

Where shall the traitor rest,
    He, the deceiver,

Who could win maiden's breast,
    Ruin, and leave her?
In the lost battle,
    Borne down by the flying,
Where mingles war's rattle
    With groans of the dying;
        Eleu loro
    There shall he be lying.

Her wing shall the eagle flap
    O'er the false-hearted;
His warm blood the wolf shall lap
    Ere life be parted:
Shame and dishonor sit
    By his grave ever;
Blessing shall hallow it
    Never, O never!
        Eleu loro
    Never, O never!

# Thomas Dibdin.

[Born 1771. Died 1841.]

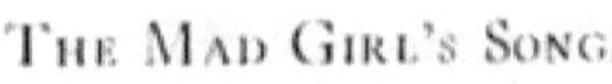

### The Mad Girl's Song.

TAKE me to your arms, love,
    For keen the wind doth blow!
O take me to your arms, love,
    For bitter is my woe.
She hears me not, she cares not,
    Nor will she list to me;
And here I lie in misery,
    Beneath the willow-tree.

My love has wealth and beauty,—
    The rich attend her door;
My love has wealth and beauty,—
    And I, alas! am poor;
The ribbon fair, that bound her hair,
    Is all that's left to me,
While here I lie, in misery,
    Beneath the willow-tree.

I once had gold and silver,—
   I thought them without end ;
I once had gold and silver,—
   I thought I had a friend.
My wealth is lost, my friend is false,
   My love is stol'n from me ;
And here I lie in misery,
   Beneath the willow-tree.

# Samuel Taylor Coleridge.

[Born 1772.    Died 1834.]

### LOVE.

ALL thoughts, all passions, all delights,
   Whatever stirs this mortal frame,
Are all but ministers of Love,
   And feed his sacred flame.

Oft in my waking dreams do I
   Live o'er again that happy hour,
When midway on the mount I lay
   Beside the ruined tower.

The moonshine stealing o'er the scene
   Had blended with the lights of eve ;
And she was there, my hope, my joy,
   My own dear Genevieve !

She leaned against the armèd man,
   The statue of the armèd knight ;
She stood and listened to my lay,
   Amid the lingering light.

Few sorrows hath she of her own,
   My hope, my joy, my Genevieve!
She loves me best whene'er I sing
   The songs that make her grieve.

I played a soft and doleful air,
   I sang an old and moving story—
An old rude song, that suited well
   That ruin wild and hoary.

She listened with a flitting blush,
   With downcast eyes and modest grace;
For well she knew, I could not choose
   But gaze upon her face.

I told her of the knight that wore
   Upon his shield a burning brand;
And that for ten long years he wooed
   The Lady of the Land.

I told her how he pined; and ah!
   The deep, the low, the pleading tone
With which I sang another's love
   Interpreted my own.

She listened with a flitting blush,
   With downcast eyes and modest grace;
And she forgave me that I gazed
   Too fondly on her face.

But when I told the cruel scorn
　That crazed that bold and lovely Knight,
And that he crossed the mountain-woods
　Nor rested day nor night ;

That sometimes from the savage den,
　And sometimes from the darksome shade,
And sometimes starting up at once
　In green and sunny glade,

There came and looked him in the face
　An angel beautiful and bright ;
And that he knew it was a Fiend,
　This miserable Knight !

And that, unknowing what he did,
　He leaped amid a murderous band,
And saved from outrage worse than death
　The Lady of the Land ;

And how she wept, and clasped his knees,
　And how she tended him in vain ;
And ever strove to expiate
　The scorn that crazed his brain ;

And that she nursed him in a cave,
　And how his madness went away,
When on the yellow forest leaves
　A dying man he lay ;

—His dying words—but when I reached
  That tenderest strain of all the ditty,
My faltering voice and pausing harp
  Disturbed her soul with pity!

All impulses of soul and sense
  Had thrilled my guileless Genevieve;
The music and the doleful tale,
  The rich and balmy eve;

And hopes, and fears that kindle hope,
  An undistinguishable throng;
And gentle wishes long subdued,
  Subdued and cherished long.

She wept with pity and delight,
  She blushed with love and virgin shame;
And like the murmur of a dream,
  I heard her breathe my name.

Her bosom heaved—she stept aside,
  As conscious of my look she stept—
Then suddenly, with timorous eye
  She fled to me and wept.

She half enclosed me with her arms,
  She pressed me with a meek embrace;
And bending back her head, looked up,
  And gazed upon my face.

15*

'Twas partly love, and partly fear,
  And partly 'twas a bashful art
That I might rather feel, than see
  The swelling of her heart.

I calmed her fears and she was calm,
  And told her love with virgin pride ;
And so I won my Genevieve,
  My bright and beauteous Bride.

## "MAID OF MY LOVE."

MAID of my love, sweet Genevieve !
  In beauty's light you glide along ;
Your eye is like the star of eve,
  And sweet your voice as Seraph's song
Yet not your heavenly beauty gives
  This heart with passion soft to glow :
Within your soul a voice there lives !
  It bids you hear the tale of woe.
When, sinking low, the sufferer wan
  Beholds no hand outstretched to save,
Fair, as the bosom of the swan
  That rises graceful o'er the wave,
I've seen your breast with pity heave,
And therefore love I you, sweet Genevieve !

# Thomas Dermody.

[Born 1774. Died 1802.]

### "Her I love."

SWEET is the woodbine's fragrant twine;
Sweet the ripe burthen of the vine;
The pea-bloom sweet, that scents the air;
The rose-bud, sweet beyond compare;
The perfume sweet of yonder grove;
Sweeter the lip of Her I love!

Soft the rich meadow's velvet green,
Where cowslip tufts are early seen;
Soft the young cygnet's snowy breast,
Or down that lines the linnet's nest;
Soft the smooth plumage of the dove;
Softer the breast of Her I love!

Bright is the star that opes the day;
Bright the mid-noon's refulgent ray;
Bright on yon hill the sunny beam;
Bright the blue mirror of the stream;
Bright the gay twinkling fires above;
Brighter the eyes of Her I love!

To match one grace, with idle pain
Through Nature's stores I search in vain;
All that is bright, and soft, and sweet,
Does in her form, concentred, meet;
Then, Muse! how weak my power must prove
To paint the charms of Her I love!

# Robert Tannahill.

[Born 1774.  Died 1810.]

### Jessie, the Flower of Dumblane.

THE sun has gone down o'er the lofty Ben-
    lomond,
    And left the red clouds to preside o'er
      the scene,
    While lonely I stray in the calm summer
      gloaming,
To muse on sweet Jessie, the Flower o' Dumblane.
How sweet is the brier with its soft faulding blossom,
    And sweet is the birk wi' its mantle of green ;
Yet sweeter and fairer, and dear to this bosom,
    Is lovely young Jessie, the Flower o' Dumblane.

She's modest as ony, and blythe as she's bonny,
    For guileless simplicity marks her its ain ;
And far be the villain, divested of feeling,
    Who'd blight in its bloom the sweet Flower o'
      Dumblane.

Sing on, thou sweet mavis, thy hymn to the e'ening,
   Thou'rt dear to the echoes of Calderwood glen;
Sae dear to this bosom, sae artless and winning,
   Is charming young Jessie, the Flower o' Dumblane.

How lost were my days till I met wi' my Jessie;
   The sports of the city seemed foolish and vain;
I ne'er saw a nymph I could ca' my dear lassie,
   Till charmed with young Jessie, the Flower o'
      Dumblane.
Though mine were the station of loftiest grandeur,
   Amidst its profusion I'd languish in pain,
And reckon as nothing the height o' its splendor,
   If wanting young Jessie, the Flower o' Dumblane.

# John Leyden, M. D.

[Born 1775.    Died 1811.]

### THE EVENING STAR.

HOW sweet thy modest light to view,
    Fair star, to love and lovers dear ;
While trembling on the falling dew
    Like beauty shining through the tear ;

Or hanging o'er that mirror-stream,
    To mark each image trembling there,
Thou seem'st to smile with softer gleam,
    To see thy lovely face so fair.

Though, blazing o'er the arch of night,
    The moon thy timid beams outshine
As far as thine each starry light,—
    Her rays can never vie with thine.

Thine are the soft, enchanting hours
    When twilight lingers on the plain,
And whispers to the closing flowers,
    That soon the sun will rise again.

Thine is the breeze that, murmuring bland
  As music, wafts the lover's sigh ;
And bids the yielding heart expand
  In love's delicious ecstasy.

Fair star, though I be doomed to prove
  That rapture's tears are mixed with pain ;
Ah ! still I feel 'tis sweet to love,—
  But sweeter to be loved again.

# Thomas Campbell.

[Born 1777.   Died 1844.]

## SONG.

DRINK ye to her that each loves best,
  And if you nurse a flame
That's told but to her mutual breast,
  We will not ask her name.

Enough, while memory tranced and glad
  Paints silently the fair,
That each should dream of joys he's had,
  Or yet may hope to share.

Yet far, far hence be jest or boast
  From hallowed thoughts so dear ;
But drink to her that each loves most,
  As she would love to hear.

# John Shaw, M. D.

[Born 1778.   Died 1809.]

### SONG.

WHO has robbed the ocean cave,
    To tinge thy lips with coral hue?
Who, from India's distant wave,
    For thee those pearly treasures drew?
        Who, from yonder orient sky,
        Stole the morning of thine eye?

Thousand charms thy form to deck,
    From sea, and earth, and air are torn;
Roses bloom upon thy cheek,
    On thy breath their fragrance borne:
        Guard thy bosom from the day,
        Lest thy snows should melt away.

But one charm remains behind,
    Which mute earth could ne'er impart;
Nor in ocean wilt thou find,
    Nor in the circling air, a heart:
        Fairest, wouldst thou perfect be,
        Take, oh take that heart from me.

# Thomas Moore.

[Born 1780.  Died 1852.]

---

### "Come, Rest in this Bosom."

COME,  rest in this bosom, my own stricken
      deer.
   Though the herd have fled from thee, thy
      home is still here ;
Here still is the smile that no cloud can o'ercast,
And a heart and a hand all thy own to the last.

Oh ! what was love made for, if 'tis not the same
Through joy and through torment, through glory and
      shame ?
I know not, I ask not, if guilt's in that heart,
I but know that I love thee, whatever thou art.

Thou hast called me thy Angel in moments of bliss,
And thy Angel I'll be, 'mid the horrors of this,
Through the furnace, unshrinking, thy steps to pursue,
And shield thee, and save thee, or perish there too.

## "Believe me."

BELIEVE me, if all those endearing young
        charms,
    Which I gaze on so fondly to-day,
    Were to change by to-morrow, and fleet in
        my arms,
    Like fairy gifts fading away,
Thou wouldst still be adored, as this moment thou art,
    Let thy loveliness fade as it will,
And around the dear ruin each wish of my heart
    Would entwine itself verdantly still.

It is not while beauty and youth are thine own,
    And thy cheeks unprofaned by a tear,
That the fervor and faith of a soul can be known,
    To which time will but make thee more dear;
No, the heart that has truly loved never forgets,
    But as truly loves on to the close,
As the sunflower turns on her god, when he sets,
    The same look which she turned when he rose.

## "The Time I've Lost."

THE time I've lost in wooing,
In watching and pursuing
    The light that lies
    In woman's eyes,
Has been my heart's undoing.
Though wisdom oft has sought me,
I scorned the lore she brought me,
    My only books
    Were woman's looks,
And folly's all they taught me.

Her smile when Beauty granted,
I hung with gaze enchanted,
    Like him the sprite
    Whom maids by night
Oft meet in glen that's haunted.
Like him, too, Beauty won me;
    If once their ray
    Was turned away,
O! winds could not outrun me.

And are those follies going?
And is my proud heart growing
  16*

Too cold or wise
For brilliant eyes
Again to set it glowing?
No—vain, alas! th' endeavor
From bonds so sweet to sever;—
Poor wisdom's chance
Against a glance
Is now as weak as ever.

----

"COULDST THOU LOOK AS DEAR."

COULDST thou look as dear as when
First I sighed for thee,
Couldst thou make me feel again
Every wish I breathed thee then,
Oh, how blissful life would be!
Hopes that now beguiling leave me,
Joys that lie in slumber cold,
All would wake, couldst thou but give me
One dear smile like those of old.

Oh, there's nothing left us now
But to mourn the past:—
Vain was every ardent vow,
Never yet did Heaven allow
Love so warm, so wild, to last.

Not even Hope could now deceive me,
  Life itself looks dark and cold;
Oh, thou never more canst give me
  One dear smile like those of old.

---

## "OH, YES—SO WELL."

OH, yes—so well, so tenderly
  Thou'rt loved, adored by me;
Fame, fortune, wealth, and liberty,
  Are worthless without thee.
Though brimmed with blisses pure and rare,
  Life's cup before me lay,
Unless thy love were mingled there
  I'd spurn the draught away.

Without thy smile, how joylessly
  All glory's meeds I see!
And even the wreath of victory
  Must owe its bloom to thee.
Those worlds for which the conqueror sighs,
  For me have now no charms;
My only world those radiant eyes,
  My throne those circling arms.

## ECHOES.

HOW sweet the answer Echo makes
　　To Music at night,
When, roused by lute or horn, she wakes,
And far away o'er lawns or lakes
　　Goes answering light!

Yet Love hath echoes truer far,
　　And far more sweet,
Than e'er, beneath the moonlight's star,
Of horn, or lute, or soft guitar,
　　The songs repeat.

'Tis when the sigh,—in youth sincere,
　　And only then,—
The sigh that's breathed for one to hear,
Is by that one, that only Dear,
　　Breathed back again.

# Allan Cunningham.

[Born 1784. Died 1842.]

### Bonnie Lady Ann.

THERE'S kames o' hinnie 'tween my luve's
    lips,
  And gowd amang her hair;
Her breists are lapt in a holy veil,
  Nae mortal een keek there.
What lips daur kiss, or what hand daur touch,
  Or what arm o' luve daur span,
The hinnie lips, the creamy lufe,
  Or the waist o' Lady Ann?

She kisses the lips o' her bonnie red rose,
  Wat wi' the blobs o' dew;
But nae gentle lip nor semple lip
  Maun touch her ladie mou.
But a broider'd belt, wi' a buckle o' gowd,
  Her jimpy waist maun span;
Oh, she's an armfu' fit for heaven—
  My bonnie Lady Ann!

Her bower casement is latticed wi' flowers
   Tied up wi' siller thread ;
And comely sits she in the midst,
   Men's longing een to feed.
She waves the ringlets frae her cheek
   Wi' her milky, milky han' ;
And her every look beams wi' grace divine,
   My bonnie Lady Ann.


The mornin' cloud is tasselt wi' gowd,
   Like my luve's broidered cap ;
And on the mantle that my luve wears
   Is many a gowden drap.
Her bonnie ee-bree's a holy arch,
   Cast by nae earthly han' ;
And the breath o' heaven is atween the lips
   O' my bonnie Lady Ann.


I wonderin' gaze on her stately steps,
   And I feed a hopeless flame ;
To my luve, alas ! she mauna stoop,
   It wad stain her honored name.
My een are bauld, they dwall on a place
   Where I daurna mint my han' ;
But I water and tend and kiss the flowers
   O' my bonnie Lady Ann.

I am her father's gardener lad,
  And puir, puir is my fa';
My auld mither gets my wee wee fee,
  With fatherless bairnies twa.
My lady comes, my lady gaes,
  Wi' a fu' and kindly han';
Oh, their blessin' maun mix wi' my luve,
  And fa' on Lady Ann!

# George Gordon, Lord Byron.

[Born 1788.   Died 1824.]

## FAREWELL!

FAREWELL! if ever fondest prayer
　For other's weal availed on high,
Mine will not all be lost in air,
　But waft thy name beyond the sky.
'Tis vain to speak, to weep, to sigh;
　Oh! more than tears of blood can tell,
When wrung from guilt's expiring eye,
　Are in the word—Farewell! Farewell!

These lips are mute, these eyes are dry;
　But in my breast, and in my brain,
Awake the pangs that pass not by,
　The thought that ne'er shall sleep again.
My soul nor deigns, nor dares complain,
　Though grief and passion there rebel;
I only know I loved in vain—
　I only feel—Farewell! Farewell!

## "When we Two parted."

WHEN we two parted
  In silence and tears,
Half broken-hearted,
  To sever for years,
Pale grew the cheek and cold,
  Colder thy kiss!
Truly that hour foretold
  Sorrow to this.

The dew of the morning
  Sunk chill on my brow,
It felt like a warning
  Of what I feel now.
Thy vows are all broken,
  And light is thy fame;
I hear thy name spoken,
  And share in its shame.

They name thee before me,
  A knell to mine ear;
A shudder comes o'er me—
  Why wert thou so dear?

They know not I know thee,
   Who know thee too well!
Long, long shall I rue thee
   Too deeply to tell.

In secret we met,
   In silence I grieve,
That thy heart would forget,
   Thy spirit deceive.
If I should meet thee
   After long years,
How should I greet thee?
   With silence and tears!

---

### "I SAW THEE WEEP."

I SAW thee weep—the big, bright tear
   Came o'er that eye of blue;
And then methought it did appear
   A violet dropping dew.
I saw thee smile—the sapphire's blaze
   Beside thee cease to shine:
It could not match the living rays
   That filled that glance of thine.

As clouds from yonder sun receive
  A deep and mellow dye,
Which scarce the shade of coming eve
  Can banish from the sky,
These smiles unto the moodiest mind
  Their own pure joy impart;
Their sunshine leaves a glow behind
  That lightens o'er the heart.

## THE HEBREW MAID.

SHE walks in beauty, like the night
  Of cloudless climes and starry skies,
And all that's best of dark and bright
  Meet in her aspect and her eyes,
Thus mellowed to that tender light
  Which heaven to gaudy day denies.

One shade the more, one ray the less,
  Had half impaired the nameless grace
Which waves in every raven tress,
  Or softly lightens o'er her face,
Where thoughts serenely sweet express
  How pure, how dear their dwelling-place.

And on that cheek and o'er that brow
So soft, so calm, yet eloquent,
The smiles that win, the tints that glow,
But tell of days in goodness spent,—
A mind at peace with all below,
A heart whose love is innocent.

---

## SONG.

THERE be none of Beauty's daughters
With a magic like thee;
And like music on the waters
Is thy sweet voice to me:
When, as if its sound were causing
The charmed ocean's pausing,
The waves lie still and gleaming,
And the lulled winds seem dreaming.

And the midnight moon is weaving
Her bright chain o'er the deep,
Whose heart is gently heaving
As an infant's asleep:
So the spirit bows before thee
To listen and adore thee;
With a full but soft emotion
Like the swell of summer's ocean.

# Maria Brooks.

---

### SONG.

DAY, in melting purple dying,
Blossoms, all around me sighing,
Fragrance, from the lilies straying,
Zephyr, with my ringlets playing,
    Ye but waken my distress;
    I am sick of loneliness.

Thou, to whom I love to hearken,
Come, ere night around me darken;
Though thy softness but deceive me,
Say thou'rt true, and I'll believe thee;
    Veil, if ill, thy soul's intent,
    Let me think it innocent!

Save thy toiling, spare thy treasure:
All I ask is friendship's pleasure;
Let the shining ore lie darkling,
Bring no gem in lustre sparkling:
    Gifts and gold are naught to me,
    I would only look on thee!

17*

Tell to thee the high-wrought feeling,
Ecstasy but in revealing ;
Paint to thee the deep sensation,
Rapture in participation,
    Yet but torture, if comprest
    In a lone, unfriended breast.

Absent still !   Ah ! come and bless me !
Let these eyes again caress thee ;
Once, in caution, I could fly thee :
Now, I nothing could deny thee ;
    In a look if death there be,
    Come, and I will gaze on thee !

# William Cullen Bryant.

[BORN 1795.]

OH, FAIREST OF THE RURAL MAIDS!

H, fairest of the rural maids!
Thy birth was in the forest shades;
Green boughs, and glimpses of the sky,
Were all that met thy infant eye.

Thy sports, thy wanderings, when a child,
Were ever in the sylvan wild;
And all the beauty of the place
Is in thy heart and on thy face.

The twilight of the trees and rocks
Is in the light shade of thy locks;
Thy step is as the wind, that weaves
Its playful way among the leaves.

Thine eyes are springs, in whose serene
And silent waters heaven is seen;

Their lashes are the herbs that look
On their young figures in the brook.

The forest depths, by foot unpress'd,
Are not more sinless than thy breast;
The holy peace that fills the air
Of those calm solitudes, is there.

# Joseph Rodman Drake, M. D.

[Born 1795.   Died 1820.]

---

## To Sarah.

ONE happy year has fled, Sall,
  Since you were all my own;
The leaves have felt the autumn blight,
  The wintry storm has blown.
We heeded not the cold blast,
  Nor the winter's icy air;
For we found our climate in the heart,
  And it was summer there.

The summer sun is bright, Sall,
  The skies are pure in hue;
But clouds will sometimes sadden them,
  And dim their lovely blue;
And clouds may come to us, Sall,
  But sure they will not stay;
For there's a spell in fond hearts
  To chase their gloom away.

In sickness and in sorrow
    Thine eyes were on me still,
And there was comfort in each glance
    To charm the sense of ill;
And were they absent now, Sall,
    I'd seek my bed of pain,
And bless each pang that gave me back
    Those looks of love again.

O, pleasant is the welcome kiss,
    When day's dull round is o'er,
And sweet the music of the step
    That meets me at the door.
Though worldly cares may visit us,
    I reck not when they fall,
While I have thy kind lips, my Sall,
    To smile away them all.

# Fitz-Greene Halleck.

[Born 1795.]

## MAGDALEN.

A SWORD, whose blade has ne'er been wet
  With blood, except of Freedom's foes ;
That hope which, though its sun be set,
  Still with a starlight beauty glows ;
A heart that worshipped in Romance
  The Spirit of the buried Time,
And dreams of knight, and steed, and lance,
  And ladye-love, and minstrel-rhyme ;
These had been, and I deemed would be
My joy, whate'er my destiny.

Born in a camp, its watch-fires bright
  Alone illumed my cradle-bed ;
And I had borne with wild delight
  My banner where Bolivar led,
Ere manhood's hue was on my cheek,
  Or manhood's pride was on my brow.

Its folds are furl'd—the war-bird's beak
  Is thirsty on the Andes now ;
I longed, like her, for other skies
Clouded by Glory's sacrifice.

In Greece, the brave heart's Holy Land,
  Its soldier-song the bugle sings ;
And I had buckled on my brand,
  And waited but the sea-wind's wings,
To bear me where, or lost or won
  Her battle, in its frown or smile,
Men live with those of Marathon,
  Or die with those of Scio's isle ;
And find in Valour's tent or tomb,
In life or death, a glorious home.

I could have left but yesterday
  The scene of my boy-years behind,
And floated on my careless way
  Wherever willed the breathing wind.
I could have bid adieu to aught
  I've sought, or met, or welcomed here,
Without an hour of shaded thought,
  A sigh, a murmur, or a tear.
Such was I yesterday—but then
I had not known thee, Magdalen.

To-day there is a change within me,
  There is a weight upon my brow,
And Fame, whose whispers once could win me
  From all I loved, is powerless now.
There ever is a form, a face
  Of maiden beauty in my dreams,
Speeding before me, like the race
  To ocean of the mountain streams—
With dancing hair, and laughing eyes,
That seem to mock me as it flies.

My sword—it slumbers in its sheath ;
  My hopes—their starry light is gone ;
My heart—the fabled clock of death
  Beats with the same low, lingering tone :
And this, the land of Magdalen,
  Seems now the only spot on earth
Where skies are blue and flowers are green ;
  And here I'd build my household hearth,
And breathe my song of joy, and twine
A lovely being's name with mine.

In vain ! in vain ! the sail is spread ;
  To sea ! to sea ! my task is there ;
But when among the unmourned dead
  They lay me, and the ocean air

Brings tidings of my day of doom,
    Mayst thou be then, as now thou art,
The load-star of a happy home;
    In smile and voice, in eye and heart,
The same as thou hast ever been,
'The loved, the lovely Magdalen.

# John Keats.

[Born 1795.   Died 1821.]

---

## Sonnet.

RIGHT star! would I were steadfast as thou
    art—
  Not in lone splendour hung aloft the night,
  And watching, with eternal lids apart,
    Like Nature's patient, sleepless Eremite,

The moving waters at their priest-like task
  Of pure ablution round earth's human shores,
Or gazing on the new soft-fallen mask
  Of snow upon the mountains and the moors:

No—yet still steadfast, still unchangeable,
  Pillowed upon my fair love's ripening breast,
To feel forever its soft fall and swell,
  Awake forever in a sweet unrest;

Still, still to hear her tender-taken breath,
And so live ever,—or else swoon to death.

# Percy Bysshe Shelley.

[Born 1795.    Died 1822.]

### Lines to an Indian Air.

ARISE from dreams of Thee,
   In the first sweet sleep of night,
When the winds are breathing low,
   And the stars are shining bright;
I arise from dreams of thee,
   And a spirit in my feet
Has led me—who knows how?
   To thy chamber-window, Sweet!

The wandering airs they faint
   On the dark, the silent stream—
The champak odours fail
   Like sweet thoughts in a dream;
The nightingale's complaint
   It dies upon her heart,
As I must die on thine,
   O belovèd as thou art!

O lift me from the grass!
  I die, I faint, I fail!
Let thy love in kisses rain
  On my lips and eyelids pale.
My cheek is cold and white, alas!
  My heart beats loud and fast;
O! press it close to thine again,
  Where it will break again at last.

------

### SONG.

FEAR thy kisses, gentle maiden;
  Thou needest not fear mine;
My spirit is too deeply laden
  Ever to burden thine.

I fear thy mien, thy tones, thy motion;
  Thou needest not fear mine;
Innocent is the heart's devotion
  With which I worship thine.

18*

## LOVE'S PHILOSOPHY.

THE fountains mingle with the river,
   And the rivers with the ocean,
The winds of heaven mix forever
   With a sweet emotion;
Nothing in the world is single,
   All things by a law divine
In one another's being mingle—
   Why not I with thine?

See the mountains kiss high heaven,
   And the waves clasp one another;
No sister flower would be forgiven
   If it disdained its brother:
And the sunlight clasps the earth,
   And the moonbeams kiss the sea—
What are all these kissings worth
   If thou kiss not me?

### SONG.

ONE word is too often profaned
   For me to profane it,
One feeling too falsely disdained
   For thee to disdain it.
One hope is too like despair
   For prudence to smother,
And Pity from thee more dear
   Than that from another.

I can give not what men call love;
   But wilt thou accept not
The worship the heart lifts above
   And the Heavens reject not:
The desire of the moth for the star,
   Of the night for the morrow,
The devotion to something afar
   From the sphere of our sorrow?

## THE FLIGHT OF LOVE.

WHEN the lamp is shattered,
   The light in the dust lies dead—
When the cloud is scattered,
   The rainbow's glory is shed.
When the lute is broken,
   Sweet tones are remembered not;
When the lips have spoken,
   Loved accents are soon forgot.

As music and splendour
   Survive not the lamp and the lute,
The heart's echoes render
   No song when the spirit is mute—
No song but sad dirges,
   Like the wind through a ruined cell,
Or the mournful surges
   That ring the dead seaman's knell.

When hearts have once mingled,
   Love first leaves the well-built nest;
The weak one is singled
   To endure what it once possessed.

O Love! who bewailest
  The frailty of all things here,
Why choose you the frailest
  For your cradle, your home, and your bier?

Its passions will rock thee,
  As the storms rock the ravens on high;
Bright reason will mock thee
  Like the sun from a wintry sky.
From thy nest every rafter
  Will rot, and thine eagle home
Leave thee naked to laughter,
  When leaves fall and cold winds come.

# Hartley Coleridge.

[Born 1796.   Died 1849.]

## SONG.

SHE is not fair to outward view,
   As many maidens be ;
Her loveliness I never knew
   Until she smiled on me.
O then I saw her eye was bright,
A well of love, a spring of light.

But now her looks are coy and cold,
   To mine they ne'er reply ;
And yet I cease not to behold
   The love-light in her eye :
Her very frowns are fairer far
Than smiles of other maidens are.

# Bryan Waller Proctor.

[Born 1796 (?).]

## SONG.

MY love is a lady of gentle line,
  Towards some like the cedar bending,
Towards me she flies, like a shape divine
  From heaven to earth descending.

Her very look is life to me,
  Her smile like the clear moon rising,
And her kiss is sweet as the honeyed bee,
  And more and more enticing.

Mild is my love as the summer air,
  And her cheek (her eyes half closing)
Now rests on her full-blown bosom fair,
  Like Languor on Love reposing.

## SONG.

HERE'S a health to thee, Mary,
    Here's a health to thee;
    The drinkers are gone,
    And I am alone,
To think of home and thee, Mary.

There are some who may shine o'er thee, Mary,
    And many as frank and free,
    And a few as fair;
    But the summer air
Is not more sweet to me, Mary.

I have thought of thy last low sigh, Mary,
    And thy dimmed and gentle eye;
    And I've called on thy name
    When the night-winds came,
And heard thy heart reply, Mary.

Be thou but true to me, Mary,
    And I'll be true to thee;
    And at set of sun,
    When my task is done,
Be sure that I'm ever with thee, Mary!

## SERENADE.

LISTEN! from the forest boughs
    The voice-like angel of the spring
Utters his soft vows
    To the proud rose blossoming.


And now beneath the lattice, dear!
    I am like thy bird complaining:
Thou above, I fear,
    Like the rose, disdaining.


From her chamber in the skies
    Shoots the lark at break of morning,
And when daylight flies
    Comes the raven's warning.


This of gloom and that of mirth
    In their mystic numbers tell;
But thoughts of sweeter birth
    Teacheth the nightingale.

# William Motherwell.

[Born 1797.  Died 1835.]

---

### Jeanie Morrison.

'VE wandered east, I've wandered west,
   Through mony a weary way !
But never, never can forget
   The luve o' life's young day.
The fire that's blawn on Beltane e'en
   May weel be black gin Yule ;
But blacker fa' awaits the heart
   Where first fond luve grows cool.

O dear, dear Jeanie Morrison,
   The thochts o' bygane years
Still fling their shadows ower my path,
   And blind my een wi' tears !
They blind my een wi' saut, saut tears,
   And sair and sick I pine,
As memory idly summons up
   The blythe blinks o' lang syne.

'Twas then we luvit ilk ither weel,
  'Twas then we twa did part;
Sweet time—sad time! twa bairns at schule,
  Twa bairns, and but ae heart!
'Twas then we sat on ae laigh bink,
  To leir ilk ither lear;
And tones, and looks, and smiles were shed,
  Remembered evermair.

I wonder, Jeanie, aften yet,
  When sitting on that bink,
Cheek touchin' cheek, loof locked in loof,
  What our wee heads could think!
When baith bent down ower ae braid page,
  Wi' ae buik on our knee,
Thy lips were on thy lesson, but
  My lesson was in thee.

Oh, mind ye how we hung our heads,
  How cheeks brent red wi' shame,
Whene'er the schule-weans laughin' said,
  We cleeked thegither hame?
And mind ye o' the Saturdays
  (The schule then skail't at noon),
When we ran off to speel the braes—
  The broomy braes o' June?

My head rins round and round about,
    My heart flows like a sea,
As ane by ane the thochts rush back
    O' schule-time and o' thee.
O mornin' life !  O mornin' luve !
    O lichtsome days and lang,
When hinnied hopes around our hearts,
    Like simmer-blossoms, sprang !


Oh, mind ye, luve, how aft we left
    The deavin' dinsome toun,
To wander by the green burnside,
    And hear its water croon ?
The simmer leaves hung ower our heads,
    The flowers burst round our feet,
And in the gloamin' o' the wud
    The throssil whusslit sweet.


The throssil whusslit in the wud,
    The burn sung to the trees,
And we, with Nature's heart in tune,
    Concerted harmonies ;
And on the knowe abune the burn
    For hours thegither sat
In the silentness o' joy, till baith
    Wi' very gladness grat.

Aye, aye, dear Jeanie Morrison,
  Tears trinkled doun your cheek,
Like dew-beads on a rose, yet nane
  Had ony power to speak !
There was a time, a blessed time,
  When hearts were fresh and young,
When freely gushed all feelings forth,
  Unsyllabled—unsung.

I marvel, Jeanie Morrison,
  Gin I hae been to thee
As closely twined wi' earliest thochts
  As ye hae been to me ?
Oh, tell me gin their music fills
  Thine ear as it does mine ;
Oh, say gin e'er your heart grows grit
  Wi' dreamings o' langsyne ?

I've wandered east, I've wandered west,
  I've borne a weary lot ;
But in my wanderings far or near,
  Ye never were forgot.
The fount that first burst frae this heart
  Still travels on its way,
And channels deeper as it rins,
  The life of luve's young day.

Oh, dear, dear Jeanie Morrison,
    Since we were sindered young,
I've never seen your face, nor heard
    The music o' your tongue ;
But I could hug all wretchedness,
    And happy could I die,
Did I but ken your heart still dreamed
    O' bygane days and me !

# James Lawson.

[Born 1799.]

---

### SONG.

WHEN Spring, arrayed in flowers, Mary,
   Danced with the leafy trees;
When larks sung to the sun, Mary,
   And hummed the wandering bees;
Then first we met and loved, Mary,
   By Grieto's louping linn;
And blither was thy voice, Mary,
   Than linties i' the whin.

Now Autumn winds blaw cauld, Mary,
   Amang the withered boughs;
And a' the bonny flowers, Mary,
   Are faded frae the knowes;
But still thy love's unchanged, Mary,
   Nae chilly Autumn there,
And sweet thy smile as Spring's, Mary,
   Thy sunny face as fair.

Nae mair the early lark, Mary,
  Trills on his soaring way;
Hushed is the lintie's sang, Mary,
  Through a' the shortening day;
But still thy voice I hear, Mary,
  Like melody divine;
Nae Autumn in my heart, Mary,
  And Summer still in thine.

# George P. Morris.

[BORN 1801.   DIED 1864.]

---

### "WHERE HUDSON'S WAVE."

WHERE Hudson's wave o'er silvery sands
  Winds through the hills afar,
Old Cronest like a monarch stands,
  Crowned with a single star!
And there, amid the billowy swells
  Of rock-ribbed, cloud-capped earth,
My fair and gentle Ida dwells,
  A nymph of mountain birth.

The snow-flake that the cliff receives,
  The diamonds of the showers,
Spring's tender blossoms, buds, and leaves,
  The sisterhood of flowers,
Morn's early beam, eve's balmy breeze,
  Her purity define;
But Ida's dearer far than these
  To this fond breast of mine.

My heart is on the hills.   The shades
  Of night are on my brow:

Ye pleasant haunts and quiet glades,
    My soul is with you now !
I bless the star-crowned highlands where
    My Ida's footsteps roam—
Oh ! for a falcon's wing to bear
    Me onward to my home.

———

## "WHEN OTHER FRIENDS."

WHEN other friends are round thee,
    And other hearts are thine ;
When other bays have crowned thee,
    More fresh and green than mine ;
Then think how sad and lonely
    This doting heart will be,
Which, while it throbs, throbs only,
    Beloved one, for thee !

Yet do not think I doubt thee,
    I know thy truth remains ;
I would not live without thee
    For all the world contains.
Thou art the star that guides me
    Along life's changing sea ;
And whate'er fate betides me,
    This heart still turns to thee.

# Edward Coate Pinkney.

[BORN 1802.   DIED 1828.]

---

## A HEALTH.

FILL this cup to one made up
    Of loveliness alone,
A woman, of her gentle sex
    The seeming paragon ;
To whom the better elements
    And kindly stars have given
A form so fair, that, like the air,
    'Tis less of earth than heaven.

Her every tone is music's own,
    Like those of morning birds,
And something more than melody
    Dwells ever in her words ;
The coinage of her heart are they,
    And from her lips each flows
As one may see the burden'd bee
    Forth issue from the rose.

Affections are as thoughts to her,
  The measures of her hours;
Her feelings have the fragrancy,
  The freshness of young flowers;
And lovely passions, changing oft,
  So fill her, she appears
The image of themselves by turns,—
  The idol of past years!


Of her bright face one glance will trace
  A picture on the brain,
And of her voice in echoing hearts
  A sound must long remain;
But memory, such as mine of her,
  So very much endears,
When death is nigh, my latest sigh
  Will not be life's, but hers.


I fill'd this cup to one made up
  Of loveliness alone,
A woman, of her gentle sex
  The seeming paragon—
Her health! and would on earth there stood
  Some more of such a frame,
That life might be all poetry,
  And weariness a name.

## SERENADE.

OOK out upon the stars, my love,
    And shame them with thine eyes,
On which, than on the lights above,
    There hang more destinies.
Night's beauty is the harmony
    Of blending shades and light ;
Then, lady, up,—look out, and be
    A sister to the night !—

Sleep not !—thine image wakes for aye
    Within my watching breast :
Sleep not !—from her soft sleep should fly,
    Who robs all hearts of rest.
Nay, lady, from thy slumbers break,
    And make this darkness gay
With looks, whose brightness well might make
    Of darker nights a day.

## SONG.

NEED not name thy thrilling name,
    Though now I drink to thee, my dear,
Since all sounds shape that magic word,
    That fall upon my ear,—Mary.

And silence, with a wakeful voice,
     Speaks it in accents loudly free,
As darkness hath a light that shows
     Thy gentle face to me,—Mary.


I pledge thee in the grape's pure soul,
     With scarce one hope, and many fears,
Mixed, were I of a melting mood,
     With many bitter tears,—Mary—
I pledge thee, and the empty cup
     Emblems this hollow life of mine,
To which, a gone enchantment, thou
     No more wilt be the wine,—Mary.


### SONG.

E break the glass, whose sacred wine
     To some beloved health we drain,
Lest future pledges, less divine,
     Should e'er the hallowed toy profane ;
And thus I broke a heart that poured
     Its tide of feelings out for thee,
In draughts, by after-times deplored,
     Yet dear to memory.

But still the old, impassioned ways
　And habits of my mind remain,
And still unhappy light displays
　Thine image chambered in my brain ;
And still it looks as when the hours
　Went by like flights of singing-birds,
Or that soft chain of spoken flowers,
　And airy gems—thy words.

## A Picture Song.

HOW may this little tablet feign
　The features of a face,
Which o'erinforms with loveliness
　Its proper share of space ;
Or human hands on ivory,
　Enable us to see
The charms that all must wonder at,
　Thou work of gods in thee !

But yet, methinks, that sunny smile
　Familiar stories tells,
And I should know those placid eyes,
　Two shaded crystal wells ;

Nor can my soul, the limner's art
   Attesting with a sigh,
Forget the blood that decked thy cheek,
   As rosy clouds the sky.

They could not semble what thou art,
   More excellent than fair,
As soft as sleep or pity is,
   And pure as mountain-air;
But here are common, earthly hues,
   To such an aspect wrought,
That none, save thine, can seem so like
   The beautiful of thought.

The song I sing, thy likeness like,
   Is painful mimicry
Of something better, which is now
   A memory to me,
Who have upon life's frozen sea
   Arrived the icy spot,
Where man's magnetic feelings show
   Their guiding task forgot.

The sportive hopes, that used to chase
   Their shifting shadows on,
Like children playing in the sun,
   Are gone—forever gone;

And on a careless, sullen peace,
  My double-fronted mind,
Like Janus when his gates were shut,
  Looks forward and behind.

Apollo placed his harp, of old,
  A while upon a stone,
Which has resounded since, when struck,
  A breaking harp-string's tone ;
And thus my heart, though wholly now
  From early softness free,
If touched, will yield the music yet
  It first received of thee.


## To H——.

THE firstlings of my simple song
  Were offered to thy name ;
Again the altar, idle long,
  In worship rears its flame.
My sacrifice of sullen years,
My many hecatombs of tears,
  No happier hours recall—

Yet may thy wandering thoughts restore
To one who ever loved thee more
    Than fickle Fortune's all.


And now, farewell!—and although here
    Men hate the source of pain,
I hold thee and thy follies dear,
    Nor of thy faults complain.
For my misused and blighted powers,
My waste of miserable hours,
    I will accuse thee not ;—
The fool who could from self depart,
And take for fate one human heart,
    Deserved no better lot.


I reck of mine the less, because
    In wiser moods I feel
A doubtful question of its cause
    And nature, on me steal—
An ancient notion, that time flings
Our pains and pleasures from his wings
    With much equality—
And that, in reason, happiness
Both of accession and decrease
    Incapable must be.

Unwise, or most unfortunate,
  My way was; let the sign,
The proof of it, be simply this—
  Thou art not, wert not mine!
For 'tis the wont of chance to bless
Pursuit, if patient, with success;
  And envy may repine,
That, commonly, some triumph must
Be won by every lasting lust.


How I have lived imports not now;
  I am about to die,
Else I might chide thee that my life
  Has been a stifled sigh;
Yes, life; for times beyond the line
Our parting traced, appear not mine,
  Or of a world gone by;
And often almost would evince,
My soul had transmigrated since.


Pass wasted flowers; alike the grave,
  To which I fast go down,
Will give the joy of nothingness
  To me, and to renown:

Unto its careless tenants, fame
Is idle as that gilded name,
    Of vanity the crown,
Helvetian hands inscribe upon
The forehead of a skeleton.


List the last cadence of a lay,
    That, closing as begun,
Is governed by a note of pain,
    O, lost and worshipped one!
None shall attend a sadder strain,
Till Memnon's statue stand again
    To mourn the setting sun,—
Nor sweeter, if my numbers seem
To share the nature of their theme.

# William Leggett.

[Born 1802.   Died 1840.]

SONG.

TRUST the frown thy features wear
　　Ere long into a smile will turn;
I would not that a face so fair
　　As thine, beloved, should look so stern.
The chain of ice that winter twines,
　　Holds not for aye the sparkling rill,
It melts away when summer shines,
　　And leaves the waters sparkling still.
Thus let thy cheek resume the smile
　　That shed such sunny light before;
And though I left thee for a while,
　　I'll swear to leave thee, love, no more.


As he who, doomed o'er waves to roam,
　　Or wander on a foreign strand,
Will sigh whene'er he thinks of home,
　　And better love his native land;

So I, though lured a time away,
    Like bees by varied sweets, to rove,
Return, like bees, by close of day,
    And leave them all for thee, my love.
Then let thy cheek resume the smile
    That shed such sunny light before,
And though I left thee for a while,
    I swear to leave thee, love, no more.

---

## To Elmira.

WRITTEN WITH FRENCH CHALK* ON A PANE OF GLASS IN
THE HOUSE OF A FRIEND.

ON this frail glass, to others' view,
    No written words appear ;
They see the prospect smiling through,
    Nor deem what secret's here.
But shouldst thou on the tablet bright
    A single breath bestow,
At once the record starts to sight
    Which only thou must know.

* The substance usually called French chalk (a variety of *talc*) has this
singular property, that what is written on glass, though easily rubbed out
again, so that no trace remains visible, by being breathed on becomes immediately distinctly legible.

Thus, like this glass, to strangers' gaze
  My heart seemed unimpressed;
In vain did beauty round me blaze,
  It could not warm my breast.
But as one breath of thine can make
  These letters plain to see,
So in my heart did love awake
  When breathed upon by thee.

# Robert Montgomery Bird, M. D.

[Born 1803. Died 1854.]

## SERENADE.

SLEEP, sleep! be thine the sleep that throws
Elysium o'er the soul's repose,
Without a dream, save such as wind,
Like midnight angels, through the mind;
While I am watching on the hill,
I, and the wailing whippoorwill.
         O whippoorwill! O whippoorwill!

Sleep, sleep! and once again I'll tell
The oft-pronounced, yet vain, farewell:
Such should his word, O maiden, be,
Who lifts the fated eye to thee;
Such should it be, before the chain
That wraps his spirit, binds his brain.
         O whippoorwill! O whippoorwill!

Sleep, sleep! the ship has left the shore,
The steed awaits his lord no more;

His lord still madly lingers by
The fatal maid he cannot fly,
And thrids the wood, and climbs the hill,
He and the wailing whippoorwill.
   O whippoorwill! O whippoorwill!

*ROBERT MONTGOMERY BIRD, M.D.* 241

# Rufus Dawes.

[Born 1803. Died 186-.]

---

## Love Unchangeable.

YES! still I love thee :—Time, who sets
 His signet on my brow,
And dims my sunken eye, forgets
 The heart he could not bow ;—
Where love, that cannot perish, grows
For one, alas! that little knows
 How love may sometimes last ;
Like sunshine wasting in the skies,
 When clouds are overcast.

The dew-drop hanging o'er the rose,
 Within its robe of light,
Can never touch a leaf that blows,
 Though *seeming* to the sight ;
And yet it still will linger there,
Like hopeless love without despair,—
 A snow-drop in the sun !
A moment finely exquisite,
 Alas! but only one.

I would not have thy married heart
  Think momently of me,—
Nor would I tear the cords apart
  That bind me so to thee;
No! while my thoughts seem pure and mild,
Like dew upon the roses wild,
  I would not have thee know,
The stream that seems to thee so still,
  Has such a tide below!

Enough! that in delicious dreams
  I see thee and forget—
Enough, that when the morning beams,
  I feel my eyelids wet!
Yet, could I hope, when Time shall fall
The darkness, for creation's pall,
  To meet thee,—and to love,—
I would not shrink from aught below,
  Nor ask for more above.

# Ralph Waldo Emerson.

[Born 1803.]

## To Eva.

H fair and stately maid, whose eyes
Were kindled in the upper skies
    At the same torch that lighted mine;
For so I must interpret still
Thy sweet dominion o'er my will,
    A sympathy divine.

Ah, let me blameless gaze upon
Features that seem at heart my own;
    Nor fear those watchful sentinels,
Who charm the more their glance forbids,
Chaste-glowing, underneath their lids,
    With fire that draws while it repels.

## THE AMULET.

YOUR picture smiles as first it smiled ;
  The ring you gave is still the same ;
Your letter tells, oh changing child !
  No tidings since it came.

Give me an amulet
  That keeps intelligence with you—
Red when you love, and rosier red,
  And when you love not, pale and blue.

Alas ! that neither bonds nor vows
  Can certify possession :
Torments me still the fear that love
  Died in its last expression.

21*

# Edmund Dorr Griffin.

[Born 1804.   Died 1830.]

### To a Lady.

LIKE target for the arrow's aim,
  Like snow beneath the sunny heats,
Like wax before the glowing flame,
  Like cloud before the wind that fleets,
I am—'tis love that made me so,
And, lady, still thou sayst me no.

The wound's inflicted by thine eyes,
  The mortal wound to hope and me,
Which naught, alas, can cicatrize,
  Nor time, nor absence, far from thee.
Thou art the sun, the fire, the wind,
That make me such; ah, then be kind!

My thoughts are darts, my soul to smite;
  Thy charms the sun, to blind my sense,
My wishes—ne'er did passion light
  A flame more pure or more intense.
Love all these arms at once employs,
And wounds, and dazzles, and destroys.

# George D. Prentice.

[Born 1804.]

TO A LADY.

THINK of thee when morning springs
  From sleep, with plumage bathed in dew,
And, like a young bird, lifts her wings
  Of gladness on the welkin blue.

And when, at noon, the breath of love
  O'er flower and stream is wandering free,
And sent in music from the grove,
  I think of thee—I think of thee.

I think of thee, when, soft and wide,
  The evening spreads her robes of light,
And, like a young and timid bride,
  Sits blushing in the arms of night.

And when the moon's sweet crescent springs
  In light o'er heaven's deep, waveless sea,
And stars are forth, like blessed things,
  I think of thee—I think of thee.

I think of thee ;—that eye of flame,
Those tresses, falling bright and free,
That brow, where " Beauty writes her name,"
I think of thee—I think of thee.

# Sir Edward Lytton Bulwer-Lytton.

[Born 1805.]

## SONG.

WHEN stars are in the quiet skies,
　Then most I pine for thee ;
Bend on me then thy tender eyes,
　As stars look on the sea.
For thoughts, like waves that glide by night,
　Are stillest when they shine,
Mine earthly love lies hushed in light
　Beneath the heaven of thine.

There is an hour when angels keep
　Familiar watch o'er men,
When coarser souls are wrapt in sleep—
　Sweet spirit, meet me then.
There is an hour when holy dreams
　Through slumber fairest glide,
And in that mystic hour it seems
　Thou shouldst be by my side.

The thoughts of thee too sacred are
　　For daylight's common beam ;
I can but know thee as my star,
　　My angel, and my dream !
When stars are in the quiet skies,
　　Then most I pine for thee ;
Bend on me then thy tender eyes,
　　As stars look on the sea.

---

## LOVE AT FIRST SIGHT.

NTO my heart a silent look
　　Flashed from thy careless eyes,
And what before was shadow, took
　　The light of summer skies.
The first-born love was in that look ;
The Venus rose from out the deep
　　Of those inspiring eyes.

My life, like some lone solemn spot
　　A spirit passes o'er,
Grew instinct with a glory not
　　In earth or heaven before.

Sweet trouble stirred the haunted spot,
And shook the leaves of every thought
    Thy presence wandered o'er!

My being yearned, and crept to thine,
    As if in times of yore
Thy soul had been a part of mine,
    Which claimed it back once more.
Thy very self no longer thine,
But merged in that delicious life,
    Which made us ONE of yore!

There bloomed beside thee forms as fair,
    There murmured tones as sweet,
But round thee breathed the enchanted air
    'Twas life and death to meet.
And henceforth thou alone wert fair,
And though the stars had sung for joy,
    Thy whisper only sweet!

# Charles Fenno Hoffman.

[Born 1806.]

## To an Autumn Rose.

TELL her I love her—love her for those eyes
  Now soft with feeling, radiant now with mirth
  Which, like a lake reflecting autumn skies,
  Reveal two heavens here to us on Earth—
The one in which their soulful beauty lies,
And that wherein such soulfulness has birth :.
Go to my lady ere the season flies,
And the rude winter comes thy bloom to blast—
Go! and with all of eloquence thou hast,
The burning story of my love discover,
And if the theme should fail, alas! to move her,
Tell her, when youth's gay budding-time is past,
And summer's gaudy flowering is over,
Like thee, my love will blossom to the last!

## THY NAME.

IT comes to me when healths go round,
   And o'er the wine their garlands wreathing
The flowers of wit, with music wound,
   Are freshly from the goblet breathing;
From sparkling song and sally gay
It comes to steal my heart away,
And fill my soul, mid festal glee,
With sad, sweet, silent thoughts of thee.

It comes to me upon the mart,
   Where care in jostling crowds is rife;
Where Avarice goads the sordid heart,
   Or cold Ambition prompts the strife;
It comes to whisper, if I'm there,
'Tis but with thee each prize to share,
For Fame were not success to me,
Nor riches wealth unshared with thee.

It comes to me when smiles are bright
   On gentle lips that murmur round me,
And kindling glances flash delight
   In eyes whose spell would once have bound
   me.

It comes—but comes to bring alone
Remembrance of some look or tone,
Dearer than aught I hear or see,
Because 'twas born or breathed by thee.

It comes to me where cloistered boughs
    Their shadows cast upon the sod;
Awhile in Nature's fane my vows
    Are lifted from her shrine to God;
It comes to tell that all of worth
I dream in heaven or know on earth,
However bright or dear it be,
Is blended with my thought of thee.

### "I will love her no more."

WILL love her no more—'tis a waste of
the heart,
This lavish of feeling—a prodigal's part :
Who, heedless the treasure a life could not
earn,
Squanders forth where he vainly may look for return.

I will love her no more ; it is folly to give
Our best years to one, when for many we live,
And he who the world will thus barter for one,
I ween by such traffic must soon be undone.

I will love her no more ; it is heathenish thus
To bow to an idol which bends not to us ;
Which heeds not, which hears not, which recks not for
aught
That the worship of years to its altar hath brought.

I will love her no more ; for no love is without
Its limit in measure, and mine hath run out ;
She engrosseth it all, and, till some she restore,
Than this moment I love her, how can I love *more?*

## THE FAREWELL.

THE conflict is over, the struggle is past,
    I have looked—I have loved—I have
        worshipped my last,
    And now back to the world, and let
        Fate do her worst
On the heart that for thee such devotion hath nursed:
To thee its best feelings were trusted away,
And life hath hereafter not one to betray.

Yet not in resentment thy love I resign;
I blame not—upbraid not—one motive of thine;
I ask not what change has come over thy heart,
I reck not what chances have doomed us to part;
I but know thou hast told me to love thee no more,
And I still must obey where I once did adore.

Farewell, then, thou loved one—O! loved but too well,
Too deeply, too blindly, for language to tell—
Farewell! thou hast trampled love's faith in the dust,
Thou hast torn from my bosom its hope and its trust!
Yet, if thy life's current with bliss it would swell,
I would pour out my own in this last fond farewell!

# James Otis Rockwell.

[Born 1807.   Died 1831.]

## To Ann.

THOU wert as a lake that lieth
  In a bright and sunny way ;
I was as a bird that flieth
  O'er it on a pleasant day ;
When I looked upon thy features,
  Presence then some feeling lent ;
But thou knowest, most false of creatures,
  With thy form thy image went.

With a kiss my vow was greeted,
  As I knelt before thy shrine ;
But I saw that kiss repeated
  On another lip than mine ;
And a solemn vow was spoken
  That thy heart should not be changed :
But that binding vow was broken,
  And thy spirit was estranged.

22*

I could blame thee for awaking
    Thoughts the world will but deride ;
Calling out, and then forsaking
    Flowers the winter wind will chide ;
Guiling to the midway ocean
    Barks that tremble by the shore ;
But I hush the sad emotion,
    And will punish thee no more.

# Nathaniel Parker Willis.

[Born 1807.]

## THE ANNOYER.

LOVE knoweth every form of air,
    And every shape of earth,
And comes, unbidden, everywhere,
    Like thought's mysterious birth.
The moonlit sea and the sunset sky
    Are written with Love's words,
And you hear his voice unceasingly,
    Like song, in the time of birds.

He peeps into the warrior's heart
    From the tip of a stooping plume,
And the serried spears, and the many men,
    May not deny him room.
He'll come to his tent in the weary night,
    And be busy in his dream,
And he'll float to his eye in morning light,
    Like a fay on a silver beam.

He hears the sound of the hunter's gun,
   And rides on the echo back,
And sighs in his ear like a stirring leaf,
   And flits in his woodland track.
The shade of the wood, and the sheen of the river,
   The cloud, and the open sky,—
He will haunt them all with his subtle quiver,
   Like the light of your very eye.


The fisher hangs over the leaning boat,
   And ponders the silver sea,
For Love is under the surface hid,
   And a spell of thought has he ;
He heaves the wave like a bosom sweet,
   And speaks in the ripple low,
Till the bait is gone from the crafty line,
   And the hook hangs bare below.


He blurs the print of the scholar's book,
   And intrudes in the maiden's prayer,
And profanes the cell of the holy man
   In the shape of a lady fair.
In the darkest night, and the bright daylight,
   In earth, and sea, and sky,
In every home of human thought
   Will Love be lurking nigh.

## To Ermengarde.

KNOW not if the sunshine waste,
    The world is dark since thou art gone!
The hours are, O! so leaden-paced!
    The birds sing, and the stars float on,
But sing not well, and look not fair;
A weight is in the summer air,
    And sadness in the sight of flowers;
And if I go where others smile,
    Their love but makes me think of ours,
And Heaven gets my heart the while.
Like one upon a desert isle,
    I languish of the dreary hours;
I never thought a life could be
So flung upon one hope, as mine, dear love, on thee!

I sit and watch the summer sky:
    There comes a cloud through heaven alone;
A thousand stars are shining nigh,
    It feels no light, but darkles on!
Yet now it nears the lovelier moon,
    And, flashing through its fringe of snow,
There steals a rosier dye, and soon
    Its bosom is one fiery glow!

The queen of life within it lies,
 Yet mark how lovers meet to part :
The cloud already onward flies,
 And shadows sink into its heart ;
And (dost thou see them where thou art ?)
 Fade fast, fade all those glorious dyes !
Its light, like mine, is seen no more,
And, like my own, its heart seems darker than before.


Where press, this hour, those fairy feet ?
 Where look, this hour, those eyes of blue ?
What music in thine ear is sweet ?
 What odour breathes thy lattice through ?
What word is on thy lip ?  What tone,
What look, replying to thine own ?
Thy steps along the Danube stray,
 Alas, it seeks an orient sea !
Thou wouldst not seem so far away,
 Flowed but its waters back to me !
I bless the slowly-coming moon,
 Because its eye looked late in thine ;
I envy the west wind of June,
 Whose wings will bear it up the Rhine ;
The flower I press upon my brow
Were sweeter if its like perfumed thy chamber now !

## THE CONFESSIONAL.

THOUGHT of thee—I thought of thee
  On ocean many a weary night,
When heaved the long and sullen sea,
  With only waves and stars in sight.
We stole along by isles of balm,
  We furled before the coming gale,
We slept amid the breathless calm,
  We flew beneath the straining sail,—
But thou wert lost for years to me,
And day and night I thought of thee!

I thought of thee—I thought of thee
  In France, amid the gay saloon,
Where eyes as dark as eyes may be
  Are many as the leaves in June:
Where life is love, and e'en the air
  Is pregnant with impassioned thought,
And song, and dance, and music are
  With one warm meaning only fraught,
My half-snared heart broke lightly free,
And, with a blush, I thought of thee!

I thought of thee—I thought of thee
  In Florence, where the fiery hearts

Of Italy are breathed away
    In wonders of the deathless arts ;
Where strays the Contadina, down
    Val d'Arno, with the song of old ;
Where clime and women seldom frown,
    And life runs over sands of gold ;
I strayed to lonely Fiesole,
On many an eve, and thought of thee.


I thought of thee—I thought of thee
    In Rome, when, on the Palatine,
Night left the Cæsar's palace free
    To Time's forgetful foot and mine ;
Or, on the Coliseum's wall,
    When moonlight touched the ivied stone,
Reclining, with a thought of all
    That o'er this scene hath come and gone,
The shades of Rome would start and flee
Unconsciously—I thought of thee.


I thought of thee—I thought of thee
    In Vallombrosa's holy shade,
Where nobles born the friars be,
    By life's rude changes humbler made.
Here MILTON framed his Paradise ;
    I slept within his very cell ;

And, as I closed my weary eyes,
  I thought the cowl would fit me well;
The cloisters breathed, it seemed to me,
Of heart's-ease—but I thought of thee.

I thought of thee—I thought of thee
  In Venice, on a night in June;
When, through the city of the sea,
  Like dust of silver, slept the moon.
Slow turned his oar the gondolier,
  And, as the black barks glided by,
The water, to my leaning ear,
  Bore back the lover's passing sigh;
It was no place alone to be,
I thought of thee—I thought of thee.

I thought of thee—I thought of thee
  In the Ionian isles, when straying
With wise ULYSSES by the sea,
  Old HOMER's songs around me playing;
Or, watching the bewitched caique,
  That o'er the star-lit waters flew,
I listened to the helmsman Greek,
  Who sung the song that SAPPHO knew:
The poet's spell, the bark, the sea,
All vanished as I thought of thee.

I thought of thee—I thought of thee
 In Greece, when rose the Parthenon
Majestic o'er the Ægean sea,
 And heroes with it, one by one ;
When, in the grove of Academe,
 Where LAIS and LEONTIUM strayed
Discussing PLATO's mystic theme,
 I lay at noontide in the shade—
The Ægean wind, the whispering tree
Had voices—and I thought of thee.

I thought of thee—I thought of thee
 In Asia, on the Dardanelles,
Where, swiftly as the waters flee,
 Each wave some sweet old story tells ;
And, seated by the marble tank
 Which sleeps by Ilium's ruins old
(The fount where peerless HELEN drank,
 And VENUS laved her locks of gold),
I thrilled such classic haunts to see,
Yet even here I thought of thee.

I thought of thee—I thought of thee
 Where glide the Bosphor's lovely waters,
All palace-lined from sea to sea :
 And ever on its shores the daughters

Of the delicious East are seen,
　Printing the brink with slippered feet,
And, O, the snowy folds between,
　What eyes of heaven your glances meet!
Peris of light no fairer be,
Yet, in Stamboul, I thought of thee.

I've thought of thee—I've thought of thee,
　Through change that teaches to forget ;
Thy face looks up from every sea,
　In every star thine eyes are set.
Though roving beneath orient skies,
　Whose golden beauty breathes of rest,
I envy every bird that flies
　Into the far and clouded West ;
I think of thee—I think of thee !
O, dearest ! hast thou thought of me ?

# Emma C. Embury.

[Born 1807.]

---

### ABSENCE.

COME to me, love; forget each sordid duty
    That chains thy footsteps to the crowded
        mart;
   Come, look with me upon earth's summer
        beauty,
    And let its influence cheer thy weary heart.
      Come to me, love!

Come to me, love; the voice of song is swelling
    From Nature's harp in every varied tone,
And many a voice of bird and bee is telling
    A tale of joy amid the forests lone.
      Come to me, love!

Come to me, love! my heart can never doubt thee,
    Yet for thy sweet companionship I pine;
Oh, never more can joy be joy without thee,
    My pleasures, even as my life, are thine.
      Come to me, love!

# Henry Wadsworth Longfellow.

[Born 1807.]

### ENDYMION.

THE rising moon has hid the stars;
Her level rays, like golden bars,
  Lie on the landscape green,
  With shadows brown between.

And silver white the river gleams,
As if Diana, in her dreams,
  Had dropped her silver bow
  Upon the meadows low.

On such a tranquil night as this,
She woke Endymion with a kiss,
  When, sleeping in the grove,
  He dreamed not of her love.

Like Dian's kiss, unasked, unsought,
Love gives itself, but is not bought;
  Nor voice, nor sound betrays
  Its deep, impassioned gaze.

23*

It comes—the beautiful, the free,
The crown of all humanity—
    In silence and alone
    To seek the elected one.

It lifts the bows, whose shadows deep
Are Life's oblivion, the soul's sleep,
    And kisses the closed eyes
    Of him, who slumbering lies.

O, weary hearts!  O, slumbering eyes!
O, drooping souls, whose destinies
    Are fraught with fear and pain,
    Ye shall be loved again!

No one is so accursed by fate,
No one so utterly desolate,
    But some heart, though unknown,
    Responds unto its own.

Responds—as if, with unseen wings,
A breath from heaven had touched its strings;
    And whispers, in its song,
    "Where hast thou stayed so long?"

# John Greenleaf Whittier.

[BORN 1808.]

## MY PLAYMATE.

THE pines were dark on Ramoth hill,
  Their song was soft and low;
The blossoms in the sweet May wind
  Were falling like the snow.

The blossoms drifted at our feet,
  The orchard birds sang clear;
The sweetest and the saddest day
  It seemed of all the year.

For, more to me than birds or flowers,
  My playmate left her home,
And took with her the laughing spring,
  The music and the bloom.

She kissed the lips of kith and kin,
  She laid her hand in mine:
What more could ask the bashful boy
  That fed her father's kine?

She left us in the bloom of May:
  The constant years told o'er
Their seasons with as sweet May morns,
  But she came back no more.

I walk, with noiseless feet, the round
  Of uneventful years;
Still o'er and o'er I sow the spring
  And reap the autumn ears.

She lives where all the golden year
  Her summer roses blow,
The dusky children of the sun
  Before her come and go.

There haply with her jewelled hand
  She smooths her silken gown,—
No more the homespun lap wherein
  I shook the walnuts down.

The wild grapes wait us by the brook,
  The brown nuts on the hill,
And still the May-day flowers make sweet
  The woods of Follymill.

The lilies blossom in the pond,
  The bird builds in the tree,
The dark pines sing on Ramoth hill
  The slow song of the sea.

I wonder if she thinks of them,
  And how the old time seems,—
If ever the pines of Ramoth wood
  Are sounding in her dreams.

I see her face, I hear her voice;
  Does she remember mine?
And what to her is now the boy
  That fed her father's kine?

What cares she that the orioles build
  For other eyes than ours,—
That other hands with nuts are filled,
  And other laps with flowers?

O playmate in the golden time!
  Our mossy seat is green,
Its fringing violets blossom yet,
  The old trees o'er it lean.

The winds so sweet with birch and fern
  A sweeter memory blow;
And there in spring the veeries sing
  The song of long ago.

And still the pines of Ramoth wood
  Are moaning like the sea,—
The moaning of the sea of change
  Between myself and thee.

# Caroline Norton.

[Born 1808.]

### Love Not.

LOVE not, love not, ye hapless sons of clay;
    Hope's gayest wreaths are made of earthly
        flowers——
Things that are made to fade and fall away,
    When they have blossomed but a few short
        hours.
      Love not, love not.

Love not, love not: the thing you love may die——
    May perish from the gay and gladsome earth;
The silent stars, the blue and smiling sky,
    Beam on its grave as once upon its birth.
      Love not, love not.

Love not, love not: the thing you love may change,
    The rosy lip may cease to smile on you;
The kindly beaming eye grow cold and strange,
    The heart still warmly beat, yet not be true.
      Love not, love not.

Love not, love not : oh ! warning vainly said,
In present years, as in the years gone by ;
Love flings a halo round the dear one's head ;
Faultless, immortal—till they change or die.
Love not, love not.

# Frederick W. Thomas.

[Born 1808.]

---

## SONG.

'TIS said that absence conquers love!
   But O! believe it not;
I've tried, alas! its power to prove,
   But thou art not forgot.
Lady, though fate has bid us part,
   Yet still thou art as dear,
As fixed in this devoted heart,
   As when I clasped thee here.

I plunge into the busy crowd,
   And smile to hear thy name;
And yet, as if I thought aloud,
   They know me still the same.
And when the wine-cup passes round,
   I toast some other fair,—
But when I ask my heart the sound,
   Thy name is echoed there.

And when some other name I learn,
    And try to whisper love,
Still will my heart to thee return,
    Like the returning dove.
In vain! I never can forget,
    And would not be forgot;
For I must bear the same regret,
    Whate'er may be my lot.


E'en as the wounded bird will seek
    Its favorite bower to die,
So, lady, I would hear thee speak,
    And yield my parting sigh.
'Tis said that absence conquers love!
    But, O! believe it not;
I've tried, alas! its power to prove,
    But thou art not forgot.

# Oliver Wendell Holmes.

[Born 1809.]

---

### STANZAS.

STRANGE! that one lightly-whispered tone
  Is far, far sweeter unto me,
Than all the sounds that kiss the earth,
  Or breathe along the sea;
But, lady, when thy voice I greet,
Not heavenly music seems so sweet.

I look upon the fair, blue skies,
  And naught but empty air I see;
But when I turn me to thine eyes,
  It seemeth unto me
Ten thousand angels spread their wings
Within those little azure rings.

The lily hath the softest leaf
  That ever western breeze hath fanned,
But thou shalt have the tender flower,
  So I may take thy hand;

That little hand to me doth yield
More joy than all the broidered field.

O, lady ! there be many things
   That seem right fair, below, above ;
But sure not one among them all
   Is half so sweet as love ;—
Let us not pay our vows alone,
But join two altars both in one.

# Anne Peyre Dinnies.

[BORN 1810.]

## WEDDED LOVE.

COME, rouse thee, dearest!—'tis not well
    To let the spirit brood
Thus darkly o'er the cares that swell
    Life's current to a flood.
As brooks, and torrents, rivers, all
Increase the gulf in which they fall,
Such thoughts, by gathering up the rills
Of lesser griefs, spread real ills,
And with their gloomy shades conceal
The landmarks Hope would else reveal.

Come, rouse thee, now—I know thy mind,
    And would its strength awaken;
Proud, gifted, noble, ardent, kind,—
    Strange thou shouldst be thus shaken!
But rouse afresh each energy,
And be what Heaven intended thee;

Throw from thy thoughts this wearying weight,
And prove thy spirit firmly great :
I would not see thee bend below
The angry storms of earthly woe.

Full well I know the generous soul
    Which warms thee into life,
Each spring which can its powers control,
    Familiar to thy wife,—
For deem'st thou she had stooped to bind
Her fate unto a *common mind?*
The eagle-like ambition, nursed
From childhood in her heart, had first
Consumed, with its Promethean flame,
The shrine—then sunk her soul to shame.

Then rouse thee, dearest, from the dream
    That fetters now thy powers :
Shake off this gloom—Hope sheds a beam
    To gild each cloud which lowers ;
And though at present seems so far
The wished-for goal—a guiding star,
With peaceful ray, would light thee on,
Until its utmost bounds be won :
That quenchless ray thou'lt ever prove
In fond, undying *Wedded Love.*

# Alfred Tennyson.

[Born 1810.]

---

### "Ask me no more."

ASK me no more: the moon may draw the sea;
The cloud may stoop from heaven and
take the shape,
With fold to fold, of mountain or of cape;
But, O too fond! when have I answered
thee?
Ask me no more.

Ask me no more: what answer should I give?
I love not hollow cheek or faded eye;
Yet, O my friend, I would not have thee die!
Ask me no more, lest I should bid thee live;
Ask me no more.

Ask me no more: thy fate and mine are sealed;
I strove against the stream, and all in vain.
Let the great river take me to the main.
No more, dear love—for at a touch I yield;
Ask me no more.

# Edgar Allan Poe.

[Born 1811.   Died 1849.]

## To —— —— ——.

I SAW thee once—once only—years ago :
I must not say how many—but not many.
It was a July midnight ; and from out
A full-orbed moon that, like thine own soul,
    soaring,
Sought a precipitant pathway up through heaven,
There fell a silvery-silken veil of light,
With quietude, and sultriness, and slumber,
Upon the upturned faces of a thousand
Roses that grew in an enchanted garden,
Where no wind dared to stir, unless on tiptoe—
Fell on the upturned faces of these roses
That gave out, in return for the love-light,
Their odorous souls in an ecstatic death—
Fell on the upturned faces of these roses
That smiled and died in this parterre, enchanted
By thee, and by the poetry of thy presence.

Clad all in white, upon a violet bank
I saw thee half reclining; while the moon
Fell on the upturned faces of the roses,
And on thine own, upturned—alas! in sorrow.

Was it not Fate that, on this July midnight—
Was it not Fate (whose name is also Sorrow)
That bade me pause before that garden-gate
To breathe the incense of those slumbering roses?
No footstep stirred: the hated world all slept,
Save only thee and me.   I paused—I looked—
And in an instant all things disappeared.
(Ah, bear in mind, this garden was enchanted!)
The pearly lustre of the moon went out:
The mossy banks and the meandering paths,
The happy flowers and the repining trees,
Were seen no more: the very roses' odours
Died in the arms of the adoring airs.
All, all expired save thee—save less than thou:
Save only the divine light in thine eyes—
Save but the soul in thine uplifted eyes.
I saw but them—they were the world to me.
I saw but them—saw only them for hours—
Saw only them until the moon went down.
What wild heart-histories seemed to lie enwritten
Upon those crystalline celestial spheres!

How dark a woe, yet how sublime a hope!
How silently serene a sea of pride!
How daring an ambition! yet how deep—
How fathomless a capacity for love!

But now, at length, dear Dian sank from sight
Into a western couch of thunder-cloud,
And thou, a ghost, amid the entombing trees
Didst glide away.   Only thine eyes remained.
They would not go—they never yet have gone.
Lighting my lonely pathway home that night,
They have not left me (as my hopes have) since.
They follow me, they lead me through the years;
They are my ministers—yet I their slave.
Their office is to illumine and enkindle—
My duty, to be saved by their bright light,
And purified in their electric fire—
And sanctified in their Elysian fire.
They fill my soul with beauty (which is hope),
And are far up in heaven, the stars I kneel to
In the sad, silent watches of my night;
While even in the meridian glare of day
I see them still—two sweetly scintillant
Venuses, unextinguished by the sun!

# Frances Sargent Osgood.

[Born 1812.   Died 1850.]

## SONG.

I LOVED an ideal—I sought it in thee;
I found it unreal as stars in the sea.

And shall I, disdaining an instinct divine—
By falsehood profaning that pure hope of mine—

Shall I stoop from my vision so lofty—so true—
From the light all Elysian that round me it threw?

Oh! guilt unforgiven, if false I could be
To myself and to Heaven, while constant to thee!

Ah no! though all lonely on earth be my lot,
I'll brave it, if only that trust fail me not—

The trust that, in keeping all pure from control
The love that lies sleeping and dreams in my soul,

It may wake in some better and holier sphere,
Unbound by the fetter Fate hung on it here!

# William H. Burleigh.

[Born 1812.]

---

### SONG.

BELIEVE not the slander, my dearest Katrine!
    For the ice of the world hath not frozen my
        heart ;
    In my innermost spirit there still is a shrine
        Where thou art remembered, all pure as
        thou art :
The dark tide of years, as it bears us along,
    Though it sweep away hope in its turbulent flow,
Cannot drown the low voice of Love's eloquent song,
    Nor chill with its waters my faith's early glow.


True, the world hath its snares, and the soul may grow
        faint
    In its strifes with the follies and falsehoods of earth ;
And amidst the dark whirl of corruption, a taint
    May poison the thoughts that are purest at birth.
Temptations and trials, without and within,
    From the pathway of virtue the spirit may lure ;

But the soul shall grow strong in its triumphs o'er sin,
  And the heart shall preserve its integrity pure.

The finger of Love, on my innermost heart,
  Wrote thy name, O adored! when my feelings were
    young;
And the record shall 'bide till my soul shall depart,
  And the darkness of death o'er my being be flung.
Then believe not the slander that says I forget,
  In the whirl of excitement, the love that was thine;
Thou wert dear in my boyhood, art dear to me yet:
  For my sunlight of life is the smile of Katrine!

# Thomas Davis.

[BORN 1814.   DIED 1845.]

## THE WELCOME.

COME in the evening, or come in the morning,
Come when you're looked for, or come without
        warning,
    Kisses and welcome you'll find here before you,
And the oftener you come here the more I'll adore you.
Light is my heart since the day we were plighted,
Red is my cheek that they told me was blighted ;
The green of the trees looks far greener than ever,
And the linnets are singing, "True lovers! don't
        sever !"


I'll pull you sweet flowers, to wear if you choose them ;
Or, after you've kissed them, they'll lie on my bosom.
I'll fetch from the mountain its breeze to inspire you ;
I'll fetch from my fancy a tale that won't tire you.
Oh! your step's like the rain to the summer-vexed
        farmer,
Or sabre and shield to a knight without armour.

I'll sing you sweet songs till the stars rise above me,
Then, wondering, I'll wish you, in silence, to love me.

We'll look through the trees at the cliff and the eyry,
We'll tread round the rath on the track of the fairy,
We'll look on the stars, and we'll list to the river,
Till you ask of your darling what gift you can give her.
Oh! she'll whisper you,—"Love as unchangeably
     beaming,
And trust, when in secret, most tunefully streaming,
Till the starlight of heaven above us shall quiver,
As our souls flow in one down eternity's river."

So come in the evening, or come in the morning,
Come when you're looked for, or come without warning,
Kisses and welcome you'll find here before you,
And the oftener you come here the more I'll adore you!
Light is my heart since the day we were plighted,
Red is my cheek that they told me was blighted;
The green of the trees looks far greener than ever,
And the linnets are singing, "True lovers! don't
     sever!"

# Henry Clapp, Junior.

[BORN 1814.]

### BLUE AND GOLD.

BY the side of the broad blue sea
  My blue-eyed maiden dwells,
  And plays with the blue-lipped shells,
  And hides in the rocky dells,
And rolls in the surf with me.

The morning with golden ray
  Would gild her beauteous head;
  But my charming blue-eyed maid
  Unloosens her golden braid,
And shames the proud light away.

The blue-bird tosses its head,
  And the violet breathes a sigh
  As my maiden passeth by;
  While to meet her dark-blue eye
The blue-bells are ever afraid.

The goldfinch with her is bold,
  And spying her radiant hair,
  He hastens to nestle him there,
  And, tuning his prettiest air,
Sings how gold ever seeketh gold.

The blue waves kiss her feet,
  And sprinkle her marble brow,
  And her blue eyes bluer grow
  Than the veins on her hand of snow,
Where the blue rivers part and meet.

And my maiden she sings to me,
  As she basks in the golden sun,
  O! lay me when life is done
  Where his goldenest rays have shone,
By the side of the broad blue sea!

# Aubrey De Vere.

[Born 1814.]

---

### Song.

BENDING between me and the taper,
  While o'er the harp her white hands strayed,
The shadows of her waving tresses
  Above my hand were gently swayed.

With every graceful movement waving,
  I marked their undulating swell;
I watched them while they met and parted,
  Curled close or widened, rose or fell.

I laughed in triumph and in pleasure,
  So strange the sport, so undesigned!
Her mother turned and asked me, gravely,
  " What thought was passing through my
    mind?"

'Tis Love that blinds the eyes of mothers,
  'Tis Love that makes the young maids fair!
She touched my hand; my rings she counted;
  Yet never felt the shadows there.

Keep, gamesome Love, beloved Infant,
  Keep ever thus all Mothers blind;
And make thy dedicated Virgins,
  In substance as in shadow, kind!

# Philip Pendleton Cooke.

[Born 1816.   Died 1850.]

### FLORENCE VANE.

LOVED thee long and dearly,
  Florence Vane;
My life's bright dream and early
  Hath come again;
I renew, in my fond vision,
  My heart's dear pain,
My hopes, and thy derision,
  Florence Vane.

The ruin, lone and hoary,
  The ruin old
Where thou didst hark my story,
  At even told,—
That spot—the hues Elysian
  Of sky and plain—
I treasure in my vision,
  Florence Vane.

Thou wast lovelier than the roses
    In their prime ;
Thy voice excelled the closes
    Of sweetest rhyme ;
Thy heart was as a river
    Without a main.
Would I had loved thee never,
    Florence Vane !

But, fairest, coldest, wonder !
    Thy glorious clay
Lieth the green sod under—
    Alas, the day !
And it boots not to remember
    Thy disdain—
To quicken love's pale ember,
    Florence Vane.

The lilies of the valley
    By young graves weep,
The daisies love to dally
    Where maidens sleep ;
May their bloom, in beauty vying,
    Never wane
Where thine earthly part is lying,
    Florence Vane !

# Epes Sargent.

[Born 1816.]

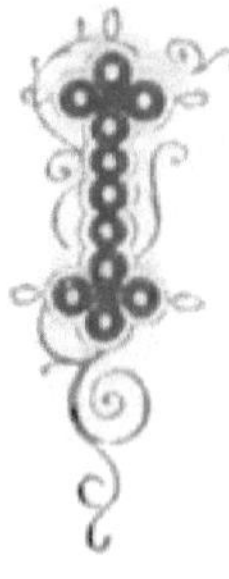

### THE FUGITIVE FROM LOVE.

IS there but a single theme
For the youthful poet's dream?
Is there but a single wire
To the youthful poet's lyre?
Earth below and heaven above —
Can he sing of naught but love?

Nay! the battle's dust I see!
God of war! I follow thee!
And, in martial numbers, raise
Worthy pæans to thy praise.
Ah! she meets me on the field —
If I fly not, I must yield.

Jolly patron of the grape!
To thy arms I will escape!
Quick, the rosy nectar bring;
" Io Bacche" I will sing.

Ha! Confusion! every sip
But reminds me of her lip.

PALLAS! give me wisdom's page,
And awake my lyric rage;
Love is fleeting; Love is vain;
I will try a nobler strain.
O, perplexity! my books
But reflect her haunting looks!

JUPITER! on thee I cry!
Take me and my lyre on high!
Lo! the stars beneath me gleam!
Here, O poet! is a theme.
Madness! She has come above!
Every chord is whispering "Love!"

# William Ross Wallace.

[Born 1818.]

## A Letter to Madeline.

PURE as a passion felt for stars;
  Deep as a thought to seraphs known;
Yet sad as bird confined to bars.
  O Madeline! my love hath grown—
  Taking a mild and solemn tone,
Yes,—still by thee my soul is stirred
  With music; from the Past it swells,
Sweet as a wave's low murmur heard
  In some old sea-remembering shells.

The misty mountains tower aloft;
  Thine infant feet their summits trod;
And in yon quiet valleys oft
  Thy little fingers from the sod
  Plucked jewels which a pitying God
Scattered around in leaf and flower,
  As if to tell each sorrowing shore,
That He who walked through Eden's bow
  Was yet the dim earth hovering o'er.

And yonder sings the silver stream—
    Dancing adown the listening hill,
That wears its mantle from the beam,
    And learns its music from the rill ;
    'Tis murmuring o'er its legends still.
While musing lonely by the scene—
    My spirit dark with grief's eclipse—
I took new heart—for Madeline
    That rill had hallowed with her lips !


Though black with Winter's shadow lies
    The land, and black with woe my soul ;
Though round me here from men and skies
    Clouds ghost-like stalk or shadowy roll,
    And *such* appears the Pilgrim's goal !—
Let but a scene which thou didst know,
    A moment meet my saddened view,
And instantly it wears a glow
    Unpressed by thee it never knew :—


Skies smile with unaccustomed spheres,
    Lit by thy memory into birth—
And fade away the doubts and fears
    That palled my heart : the very earth,
    So dark before, trembles with mirth ;
While through her everlasting plains

The rivers broad triumphing roll,
As if they warmed her swelling veins,
    And thought she owned a living soul.

Thus hourly do I feel a chain,
    Whose links are wreathed with flowers and
        light,
Is doomed forever to remain
    Between the world and me :—Thy plight,
    The beautiful star-gush of a night,
Whose dusk wings rustle sadly round—
    Thy love—a pure flame lit about,
Which must in Nature's Vase* be found,
    To bring its loveliest colours out.

---

* The vase was of pure alabaster, whose best figures only appeared when
a lamp was kindled inside.—*Eastern Travels.*

# Thomas Dunn English, M. D.

[Born 1819.]

## GOOD-NIGHT.

MY dear, good-night! the moon is down,
　　The stars have brighter grown above;
There's quiet in this dusky town,
　　And all things slumber, save my love.
Good-night! good-night! and in thy dreams
　　Go wander in a pleasant clime,
By greenest meadows, singing streams,
　　And seasons all one summer time—
　　Good-night, my dear, good-night!

My love, good-night! let slumber steep
　　In poppy-juice those melting eyes,
Till morn shall wake thee from thy sleep,
　　And bid my spirit's dawn arise.
Good-night! good-night! and as to rest
　　Upon thy couch thou liest down,
One throb for me pervade thy breast,
　　And then let sleep thy senses drown.
　　Good-night, my love—good night!

## THE EARL'S DAUGHTER.

I WOULD not care to see thee—thou
   Art changed, they tell me—so am I ;
More bronzed my visage, somewhat tamed
   The spirit once so high.
   And if of beauty less
      Than once thou hadst, thou hast,
   Let me alone behold
      Thy features in the past—
      Be as I saw thee last.


For as within that past they were,
   Thy charms by memory here are limned—
The tremulous nostril, rounded chin,
   Bright eye that never dimmed,
   And snooded, waving hair
      Which ripple-marked a shore
   Whose beach was ivory—
      Unhappy me forlore,
      My bark rides there no more.


What time we walked by Avon's side,
   Our spirits twain combined in one,
And dreamed of lands with Spring eterne,

And never-setting sun—
This is no longer ours;
  I wander to and fro,
Dejected, blind, and shorn;
    The sunlight will not glow;
    Hope ever answers—" No !"


For I am poor.   Within that word
  How many grievous faults there lay;
Such has been since old Babylon,
  And such shall be for aye.
Yet not thy acres broad,
    Thy vassals nor thy gold,
Me in such strong control
    Had ever power to hold,
    As thy charms manifold.


Thou art the daughter of an earl,
  Whose ancestor at Azincour
Fell, fighting by his monarch's side,
  When mine was but a boor.
Since then a host of lords
    And dames of high degree
Gave lustre to thy line,
    Till birth and dignity
    Rose to their height in thee.

Yet, azure-blooded as thou art,
  Whilst I am come of lowlier race,
I did not once thy lineage
  Within thy beauty trace.
  I scanned no pedigree
    Thy loveliness to prize;
  I read no Domesday Book,
    In love to make me wise;
    High rank fanned not my sighs.

But thou, whilst sitting in the shade
  Of thine old famous family tree,
Wilt scarcely to thy mind recall
  One, once so much to thee.
  So high thy station now,
    Thy vision's careless sweep
  Falls not below to strike
    That vastly lower deep,
    Wherein I ever creep.

Thou wert one time all tenderness,
  With passion glowing like a spark——
Sole ember in those ashes grey——
  Which flashed, and all grew dark.
  The coolness of thy pride
    Forbade to rise to fire
      26*

What should have been a flame,
    And swelled and mounted higher,—
    But *I* did not expire.


*I* lived—I live, if that be life
    To drag these weary moments thus,
Doomed to a lack of loving, when
    Of love most covetous.
    I am that which I was,
      But thou art different grown,
    Chilled, petrified by rank,
      Thyself a thing of stone,
      Emotionless, alone.


They wonder at thy scorn of men,
    The trembling vassals of thy nod;
They see not as thy pinions sweep,
    Where once thy footsteps trod.
    And thou midst flattering peers
      Mayst well, perhaps, forget
    How dearer once I was
      Than all the jewels set
      Thick on thy coronet.


But *I* remember—'tis to me
    Fixed as a Median edict; would

The past might verily pass, and I
  Forget thee as I should.
Still for thy love I yearn,
    Although 'tis not for me;
As well the pond expect
    To mingle with the sea,
    As I to mate with thee.


These are my final words to thee—
  Years part me from the timid first—
They gushed when came this flood of tears,
  Or else this heart had burst.
  These uttered, none shall know,
    Save Him who knows all things,
  How, driven to my heart
    On barbed arrow's wings,
    This hopeless passion stings.

## HER SINGING.

AFAR  I stood and listened
    To hear my darling sing—
With every note that heaved her throat,
    Her eyes of violet glistened—
        Pretty thing!

The breeze, with will capricious,
    Blew fastly through the trees—
It drove away the ditty gay,
    Whose notes were so delicious—
        Wicked breeze!

To still the maiden's singing
    It acts a fruitless part;
I hear no words, but, like a bird's,
    The notes she made are ringing
        Through my heart.

## O'er the Seas.

FAINT streams the shimmer of the moon
  Through yonder lattice pane;
The quiet of the night enfolds
  My mourning soul again.
Deep shadows from the hills depend,
  And fall from yonder trees:—
How turns my heart from these to thee,
  Fair lady, o'er the seas!

I own no land, I hold no rank,
  I labour for my bread;
These hands of mine are hard with toil,
  And heavy falls my tread.
Were I to speak my thoughts, thy frown
  My bold desires would freeze;
And yet I turn from toil to thee,
  Fair lady, o'er the seas.

The troubadours of old could sing
  How strove, and not in vain,
A serf, by deeds of high emprise,
  A demoiselle to gain.

The age is one which does not know
    Such idle tales as these,
Yet still I turn with hope to thee,
    Fair lady, o'er the seas.

The moon is down, and all is dark ;
    The clouds are o'er the skies ;
Sleep falls on other things around,
    But shuns these wakeful eyes.
Through darkness ever so profound
    The eye of memory sees ;
From gloom my spirit turns to thee,
    Fair lady, o'er the seas.

Light let the breezes waft the barque
    Wherein my darling sails ;
Smile over her the bluest skies,
    Blow round her spicy gales.
Bring back my love to walk again
    Beneath the oaken trees ;
Come back ! from other lands, come back,
    Fair lady, o'er the seas !

# James Russell Lowell.

[Born 1819.]

## SONG.

LIFT up the curtains of thine eyes
  And let their light outshine!
Let me adore the mysteries
  Of those mild orbs of thine,
Which ever queenly calm do roll,
Attunèd to an ordered soul!

Open thy lips yet once again,
  And, while my soul doth hush
With awe, pour forth that holy strain
  Which seemeth me to gush,
A fount of music, running o'er
From thy deep spirit's inmost core!

The melody that dwells in thee
  Begets in me as well
A spiritual harmony,
  A mild and blessed spell;
Far, far above earth's atmosphere
I rise, whene'er thy voice I hear.

# 𝔄. 𝔐. 𝔍𝔡𝔢, 𝔍𝔲𝔫𝔦𝔬𝔯.

[Born 1825.]

---

### The Nameless River.

NOW, azure as the crystal air,
 Now, like unsullied snows,
In yonder valley, shining there,
 A nameless river flows.

Adown the rocks in bright cascades
 It pours its flood of song ;
Through fragrant fields and silent shades
 Its waters wind along.

Flowers blossom on the rock-crowned hills
 Whence its fair currents glide,
And overhang the woodland rills
 That swell its stately tide.

Serene its radiant waters flow
 In valleys calm and deep,
Where pine and evergreen cedar grow,
 And bending willows weep.

Beautiful flowers its banks adorn,
  Its waves are lily-crowned,
And harvests of the emerald corn
  Swell o'er the plains around.

Yet not for this, forevermore
  I love its silvery tide;
My steadfast, peerless ISIDORE
  Dwells on the river-side!

Upon its grassy banks at noon,
  Like one in dreams astray,
I listen to the tremulous tune
  The gliding waters play.

Still unto her my spirit leans,
  When, by the river-side,
Mid fragrant flowers and evergreens
  I walk at eventide.

I loiter by its waves at night,
  Through shadowy vales afar,
With visions of ideal delight
  Entranced as lovers are.

With tremulous stars the waters shine
  Like old enchanted streams :—
Beneath her lattice, wreathed with vine,
  They murmur whilst she dreams!

Flow on, thou nameless river! flow
  In beauty to the sea;
My heart is on thy waves of snow,
  My love flows on with thee.

Thy silent waves to me no more
  Like nameless waters glide,—
I name thee from my ISIDORE,
  Who dwells upon thy side!

# James Bayard Taylor.

[Born 1825.]

### BEDOUIN SONG.

FROM the Desert I come to thee
On a stallion shod with fire ;
And the winds are left behind
In the speed of my desire.
Under thy window I stand,
And the midnight hears my cry :
I love thee, I love but thee,
With a love that shall not die
Till the sun grows cold,
And the stars are old,
And the leaves of the Judgment
Book unfold !

Look from thy window and see
My passion and my pain ;
I lie on the sands below,
And I faint in thy disdain.

Let the night-winds touch thy brow
With the heat of my burning sigh,
And melt thee to hear the vow
Of a love that shall not die
Till the sun grows cold,
And the stars are old,
And the leaves of the Judgment
Book unfold!

My steps are nightly driven,
By the fever in my breast,
To hear from thy lattice breathed
The word that shall give me rest.
Open the door of thy heart,
And open thy chamber door,
And my kisses shall teach thy lips
The love that shall fade no more
Till the sun grows cold,
And the stars are old,
And the leaves of the Judgment
Book unfold!

## SONG.

THE violet loves a sunny bank,
    The cowslip loves the lea ;
The scarlet creeper loves the elm,
    But I love—thee !

The sunshine kisses mount and vale,
    The stars they kiss the sea ;
The west winds kiss the clover bloom,
    But I kiss—thee !

The oriole weds his mottled mate ;
    The lily's bride o' the bee ;
Heaven's marriage-ring is round the earth—
    Shall I wed thee ?

## PHANTOMS.

GAIN I sit within the mansion,
  In the old, familiar seat ;
And shade and sunshine chase each other
  O'er the carpet at my feet.

But the sweet-brier's arms have wrestled
      upwards
  In the summers that are past,
And the willow trails its branches lower
  Than when I saw them last.

They strive to shut the sunshine wholly
  From out the haunted room ;
To fill the house, that once was joyful,
  With silence and with gloom.

And many kind, remembered faces
  Within the doorway come—
Voices, that wake the sweeter music
  Of one that now is dumb.

They sing, in tones as glad as ever,
  The songs she loved to hear ;

They braid the rose in summer garlands,
  Whose flowers to her were dear.

And still, her footsteps in the passage,
  Her blushes at the door,
Her timid words of maiden welcome,
  Come back to me once more.

And all forgetful of my sorrow,
  Unmindful of my pain,
I think she has but newly left me,
  And soon will come again.

She stays without, perchance, a moment,
  To dress her dark-brown hair;
I hear the rustle of her garments—
  Her light step on the stair!

O, fluttering heart! control thy tumult,
  Lest eyes profane should see
My cheeks betray the rush of rapture
  Her coming brings to me!

She tarries long: but lo, a whisper
  Beyond the open door,
And, gliding through the quiet sunshine,
  A shadow on the floor!

Ah ! 'tis the whispering pine that calls me ;
   The vine, whose shadow strays ;
And my patient heart must still await her,
   Nor chide her long delays.

But my heart grows sick with weary waiting,
   As many a time before :
Her foot is ever at the threshold,
   Yet never passes o'er.

# Richard Henry Stoddard.

[Born 1825.]

## A Serenade.

THE moon is muffled in a cloud,
    That folds the lover's star,
But still beneath thy balcony
    I touch my soft guitar.

If thou art waking, Lady dear,
    The fairest in the land,
Unbar thy wreathèd lattice now,
    And wave thy snowy hand.

She hears me not; her spirit lies
    In trances mute and deep;—
But Music turns the golden key
    Within the gate of Sleep!

Then let her sleep, and if I fail
    To set her spirit free,
My song shall mingle in her dream,
    And she will dream of me!

# Joseph Brennan.

[Born 1828.   Died 1857.]

## TO MY WIFE.

COME to me, dearest—I'm lonely without thee;
Day-time and night-time I'm thinking about
    thee;
Night-time and day-time in dreams I behold
    thee—
Unwelcome the waking that ceases to fold thee.
Come to me, darling, my sorrows to lighten;
Come in thy beauty, to bless and to brighten;
Come in thy womanhood, meekly and lowly;
Come in thy lovingness, queenly and holy.

Swallows will flit round the desolate ruin,
Telling of Spring and its joyous renewing;
And thoughts of thy love, and its manifold treasure,
Are circling my heart with a promise of pleasure.
Oh, Spring of my spirit! oh, May of my bosom!
Shine out on my soul till it bourgeon and blossom:
The waste of my life has a rose-root within it,
And thy fondness alone to the sunshine can win it.

Figure that moves like a song through the even—
Features lit up by a reflex of Heaven—
Eyes like the skies of poor Erin, our mother,
Where shadow and sunshine are chasing each other;
Smiles coming seldom, but childlike and simple,
Opening their eyes from the heart of a dimple;
Oh, thanks to the Saviour; that even thy seeming
Is left to the exile to brighten his dreaming.

You have been glad when you knew I was gladdened;
Dear, are you sad now to hear I am saddened?
Our hearts ever answer in tune and in time, love,
As octave to octave, and rhyme unto rhyme, love.
I cannot weep, but your tears will be flowing;
You cannot smile, but my cheeks will be glowing;
I would not die without you at my side, love;
You will not linger when I shall have died, love.

Come to me, dear, ere I die of my sorrow,
Rise on my gloom like the sun of to-morrow—
Strong, swift, and fond as the words which I speak, love,
With a song on your lips and a smile on your cheek, love.
Come, for my heart in your absence is weary;
Haste, for my spirit is sickened and dreary;
Come to the heart which is throbbing to press thee;
Come to the arms that would fondly caress thee.

# John Esten Cooke.

[Born 1830.]

## THE BRIDE OF THE CHEVALIER.

### I.

A LUCKY man is the Chevalier,
  The Chevalier Louis D'Or;
He won my beautiful love from me;
  He was rich—I very poor:
    So very poor that the prudent maid,
When we were weighed in the scales together,
Found the one side heavy as lead,
    My own as light as a feather!

What then were the loves of boy and girl
  Who had played for years 'neath the oak-trees tall,
And plighted their troth a thousand times,
  —When the Chevalier came to the hall?
He came in a chariot gay and fine,
  I, through the dust of the common way;
'Twas a silly thought that a woman's heart
  Could say the rich man nay.

He made his elegant bow, and smiled ;
    He came again and the day was won :
When a month had passed he was there no more,
    And the light from the hall was gone :
The light and life of the house and lawn
    Had disappeared with the form so dear ;
My pride and joy, my hope, my all,
    Was the bride of the Chevalier !


And now, good friend, do you ask again,
    Why *woman* with me is a word of scorn ?
I loved this girl with a doting love,
    And she made my life forlorn !
She sold her maiden body and soul
    For silks and jewels, and plate and gold :
Faith, and truth, and honor, and heart
    —Sold, sold, sold !


The false and feeble heart gave way ;
    She made me the man you see me now—
With the silver in my youthful hair
    And the furrows here on my brow :
She taught me then, in my early youth,
    That women were false, and weak, and mean :
If she had clung to her troth—who knows—
    My life—what it might have been ?
    28

For Spring was then in the bud with me ;
   My father left me a noble name—
With love to shine on the rugged path,
   I looked to the heights of fame :
And now——I ponder, and mope and dream
   Through a weary life that I hate, my friend,
And but for fear of the coward's hiss
   At a coward's act, would end !

Do you think I envy the Chevalier
   His beautiful bride with the sunny curls—
The woman I loved with a foolish love—
   Adored as the pearl of pearls ?
The Chevalier is prince of the Town,
   But I am king of the world of Thought—
He is welcome, for me, as the flowers in May,
   To the bride whom his money bought !

And she, with a soul that loved alone
   The red gold's sheen, and the back low bent
To the gilded coach—is welcome too ;
   She may reign to her heart's content ;
She loved me once, if she does not now,
   When a freezing stare would greet my claim
To an old acquaintance, years ago,
   With the splendid city dame !

### II.

These words I said with a bitter heart,
  And thought with scorn of the laughing queen,
As I walked, with a scowl, through the smiling woods,
  And over the meadows green ;—
But when I met, at a ball last night,
  The beautiful bride of the Chevalier,
You may laugh, but I swear, at sight of me,
  Her eye was dim with a tear !

Does she think—I said—in the dance's whirl,
  As she sees me here, of the hours long gone—
The hours we spent in the dear old hall,
  And under the oaks on the lawn ?
I turned away, for the dance was done,
  I turned away with a bitter heart—
But a slender finger touched my arm—
  We walked from the crowd apart.

Shall I write the words of the voice that shook,
  As the blue eyes filled with a sudden tear ?
The words would scarcely bring a smile
  To the lips of the Chevalier !
" Alas ! for the days," were the murmured words,
  " We passed in the hall, by the sunny stream,
The old, old days come back to me,
  Like a happy, smiling dream !

"And you—you have never married, sir—
  You do not love me—I see that well:
You pity me, or perhaps despise
  The married ball-room belle!
But oh! if you knew why the blaze and din
  Of balls is all that I live for now—
You would know that the pearls that loop my hair
  Droop over a burning brow!

"I have pined, long years, for the present hour—
  I have tried, with a trembling hand, to write;
But the time has come; we are face to face,
  You shall know the truth to-night!"
And the truth, the terrible, awful truth,
  I heard from the lips that were yet so dear:
She had loved me still, with her heart of hearts,
  When the bride of the Chevalier.

A guardian's threat, and a feeble will,
  Had made her yield to the awful shame—
She told me all with a writhing lip
  And a cheek that burned like flame.
She told me all, as I shuddered there;
  She begged like a child for a word of grace—
From me who longed to draw her close
  In a passionate, wild embrace!

But the madness passed, and I said no more
  Than the simple words I write down here,—
" I love you, my darling, and pardon all,"
  Then I bowed to the Chevalier :
She took his arm with a smothered sigh
  And a look so sad as they passed away,
That the blue eyes wet with tears will haunt
  My heart to its dying day.


And so, I have told, good friend of mine,
  The story the world has got by heart.
I do not mutter against my fate,
  For each must play his part :
For me, I have worn the " inky cloak "
  While you may have danced in ribbons gay ;
But the dress is naught so the heart is right,
  And we watch, and praise, and pray !

# Edward Robert Bulwer-Lytton.

[Born 1831.]

## At Paris.

AT Paris it was, at the opera there,
    And she looked like a queen in a book that
        night,
    With the wreath of pearl in her raven hair,
      And the brooch on her breast so bright.

Of all the operas Verdi wrote,
    The best to me is the Trovatore,
And Mario could charm with his tenor note
    The souls in Purgatory.

The moon on the tower slept soft as snow ;
    And who was not thrilled in the strangest way,
As we heard him sing, while the gas burned low,
    " Non ti scordar di me ?"

There, in our front-row box, we sat
    Together, my bride-betrothed and I—

My gaze was fixed on my opera-hat,
    And hers on the stage hard by.

Meanwhile I was thinking of my first love,
    As I had not been thinking of aught for years,
Till over my eyes there began to move
    Something that felt like tears.

I thought of the dress that she wore last time,
    When we stood 'neath the cypress-trees together,
In that lost land, in that soft clime,
    In the crimson evening weather.

I thought of our little quarrels and strife,
    And the letter that brought me back my ring ;
And it all seemed then, in the waste of life,
    Such a very little thing.

And I think, in the lives of most women and men,
    There's a moment when all would go smooth and
        even,
If only the dead could find out when
    To come back and be forgiven.

# Paul H. Hayne.

[Born 1831.]

---

## A Portrait.

THE laughing Hours before her feet
    Are strewing vernal roses,
And the voices in her soul are sweet
    As music's mellowed closes ;
All hopes and passions heavenly-born,
    In her have met together,
And joy diffuses round her morn
    A mist of golden weather.


As o'er her cheek of delicate dyes
    The blooms of childhood hover,
So do the tranced and sinless eyes
    All childhood's heart discover—
Full of a dreamy happiness
    With rainbow fancies laden,
Whose arch of promise glows to bless
    Her spirit's beauteous Aidenn.

She is a being born to raise
  Those undefiled emotions,
That link us with our sunniest days
  And most sincere devotions ;
In her, we see renewed, and bright,
  That phase of earthly story,
Which glimmers in the morning light
  Of God's exceeding glory.

Why in a life of mortal cares
  Appear these heavenly faces ?
Why on the verge of darkened years
  These amaranthine graces ?
'Tis but to cheer the soul that faints
  With pure and blest evangels,
To prove if heaven is rich with saints,
  That earth may have her angels.

Enough ! 'tis not for me to pray
  That on her life's sweet river,
The calmness of a virgin day
  May rest, and rest forever ;
I know a guardian genius stands
  Beside those waters lowly,
And labours with immortal hands
  To keep them pure and holy.

# George Arnold.

[Born 1834.]

## SERENADE.

HEAR the dry-voiced insects call,
   And " Come !" they say, " the night grows
      brief !"
I hear the dew-drops pattering fall
   From leaf to leaf—from leaf to leaf.

Your night-lamp glimmers fitfully ;
   I watch below ; you sleep above ;
Yet on your blind I seem to see
   Your shadow, Love—your shadow, Love !

The roses in the night-wind sway,
   Their petals glistening with the dew ;
As they are longing for the day,
   I long for you—I long for you !

But you are in the land of dreams ;
   Your eyes are closed ; your gentle breath
So faintly comes, your slumber seems
   Almost like Death—almost like Death !

Sleep on ; but may my music twine
    Your sleep with strands of melody,
And lead you, gentle Love of mine,
    To dream of me—to dream of me !

---

## JAM SATIS.

NOT much for sordid golden dross I care,
    I wish not much of worldly wealth to hold ;
Seek her I love—look on her shining hair—
    Is it not wealth of gold ?

I am not envious of the diamond's flash,
    Its wondrous brilliance dazzleth not my sight,
For her sweet eyne, beneath their fringèd lash,
    Make dim the diamond's light.

I care no more for music's dreamy swell,
    Nor flute nor viol greatly pleaseth me ;
Her speech is softer than a silver bell,
    Her laugh is melody.

I leave the wine which once I loved to sip ;
    Why should I drain the crimson beaker dry,
When there is subtile nectar on her lip
    That I may drink, and die ?

# Nathaniel G. Shepherd.

[Born 1836.]

A Summer Reminiscence.

HEAR no more the locust beat
   His shrill loud drum through all the day;
I miss the mingled odours sweet
   Of clover and of scented hay.

No more I hear the smothered song
   From hedges guarded thick with thorn:
The days grow brief, the nights are long,
   The light comes like a ghost at morn.

I sit before my fire alone,
   And idly dream of all the past:
I think of moments that are flown—
   Alas! they were too sweet to last.

The warmth that filled the languid noons—
   The purple waves of trembling haze—
The liquid light of silver moons—
   The summer sunset's golden blaze.

I feel the soft winds fan my cheek,
  I hear them murmur through the rye;
I see the milky clouds that seek
  Some nameless harbour in the sky.

The stile beside the spreading pine,
  The pleasant fields beyond the grove,
The lawn where, underneath the vine,
  She sang the song I used to love.

The path along the windy beach,
  That leaves the shadowy linden-tree,
And goes by sandy capes that reach
  Their shining arms to clasp the sea.

I view them all—I tread once more
  In meadow grasses cool and deep;
I walk beside the sounding shore,
  I climb again the wooded steep.

Oh, happy hours of pure delight!
  Sweet moments drowned in wells of bliss!
Oh, halcyon days so calm and bright—
  Each morn and evening seemed to kiss!

And that whereon I saw her first,
  While angling in the noisy brook,
When through the tangled wood she burst;
  In one small hand a glove and book,

As with the other, dimpled, white,
  She held the slender boughs aside ;
While through the leaves the yellow light
  Like golden water seemed to glide,

And broke in ripples on her neck,
  And played like fire around her hat,
And slid adown her form to fleck
  The moss-grown rock on which I sat.

She standing rapt in sweet surprise,
  And seeming doubtful if to turn ;
Her novel, as I raised my eyes,
  Dropped down amid the tall green fern.

This day and that—the one so bright,
  The other like a thing forlorn ;
To-morrow, and the early light
  Will shine upon her marriage morn.

For when the mellow autumn flushed
  The thickets where the chestnut fell,
And in the vales the maple blushed,
  Another came who knew her well,

Who sat with her below the pine,
  And with her through the meadow moved,
And underneath the purpling vine
  She sang to him the song I loved.

# Thomas Bailey Aldrich.

[Born 1836.]

## "Madam, as you pass us by."

MADAM, as you pass us by,
   Dreaming of your loves and wine,
Do not brush your rich brocade
   Against this little maid of mine,
Madam, as you pass us by.

When in youth my blood was warm;
   Wine was royal, life complete;
So I drained the flask of wine,
   So I sat at women's feet,
When in youth my blood was warm.

Time has taught me pleasant truths:
   Lilies grow where thistles grew;
Ah, you loved me not.   This maid
   Loves me.   There's an end of you!
Time has taught me pleasant truths.

I will speak no bitter words,
　　Too much passion made me blind;
You were subtle.　Let it go!
　　For the sake of womankind
I will speak no bitter words.

But, Madam, as you pass us by,
　　Dreaming of your loves and wine,
Do not brush your rich brocade
　　Against this little maid of mine,
Madam, as you pass us by.

# INDEX OF SUBJECTS.



29*

# INDEX OF FIRST LINES.

# INDEX OF AUTHORS.



Dr. Akenside was born at Newcastle-on-Tyne, England, on November 9, 1721, and was educated at the University of Edinburgh. He took his degree of Doctor of Medicine at the University of Leyden, May 16, 1744. He was a Fellow of the Royal Society; Cambridge conferred on him the degree of M. D.; he became Physician to the St. Thomas's Hospital, and afterwards to the Queen; and was a Fellow of the College of Physicians. He wrote numerous medical essays, but is chiefly known as the author of the "Pleasures of the Imagination." He died June 23, 1770.



Thomas Bailey Aldrich was born at Portsmouth, in New Hampshire, in 1836, and was educated for the mercantile profession. This he has abandoned for general literature. He has published several books of Tales and Poems, and is a contributor to the various magazines and journals.



Of Richard Allison we can learn nothing. The poem quoted is taken from "An Houre's Recreation in Musicke," 1606.



There are two poems of unknown authorship in this collection. Of one of these, "Helen of Kirkconnell," there are several versions. We have selected that which we think to be the most correct. "Waly, waly!" is more modern than the other poem; and it has been asserted to have for its heroine Lady Barbara Erskine, wife of the second Marquis of Douglass. The allusions in the second and fifth stanzas are not, however, consistent with the story of the Marchioness. Our version is from the "Tea-table Miscellany," 1724.



George Arnold was born in the city of New York, on June 24, 1834, and received his education at home, under the direction of his parents, who were persons of refined and cultivated tastes. His boyhood was passed in Southern Illinois, but he returned to New York before arriving at manhood, and there engaged in literature, about 1856. He has been connected editorially with the press, and has contributed largely to the journals and magazines, his productions being principally poems, tales, and sketches of humorous or ideal character.



FRANCIS ATTERBURY, Bishop of Rochester, was born at Newport-Pagnel, in Buckinghamshire, England, on March 6, 1662, and was educated at Christ Church College, Oxford, where he took the degree of Master of Arts, in 1687. He was appointed one of the chaplains-in-ordinary to William and Mary. He early engaged in religious controversial literature, and one of his pamphlets on the High-Church side provoked the ire of Burnet. The lower House of Convocation, in whose behalf he wrote, sent a commendatory letter to Oxford on his behalf, which obtained for him the degree of Doctor of Divinity. In 1700 he was made Archdeacon of Totness, and was appointed by Queen Anne, in 1702, one of her chaplains; in 1704, Dean of Carlisle; in 1707, Canon Residentiary of Exeter; and in 1709, Preacher of the Rolls Chapel. In 1710, he was unanimously chosen Prolocutor of the lower House of Convocation. In 1712 he was made Dean of Christ Church; and in 1713, Bishop of Rochester, and Dean of Westminster. In August, 1722, he was arrested and committed to the Tower, on suspicion of being concerned in a plot in favor of the Pretender. A bill of pains and penalties was passed in his case, May 27th, 1722–3; and on the 18th of June, he embarked on board the Aldborough man-of-war, and was landed at Calais the Friday following. He resided at Paris until his death, which occurred February 17, 1731.



ROBERT AYTOUN was born at Fifeshire, Scotland, in 1590. He was knighted, and made Gentleman of the Bedchamber by Charles the First, and afterwards private secretary to the Queen. He died in 1638.



Of RICHARD BARNEFIELD little is known, except that his writings appeared between 1594 and 1598. The poem we have quoted from him was for a long time, and is frequently still, erroneously attributed to Shakspeare.



ROBERT MONTGOMERY BIRD was born in 1803, and was educated at Philadelphia, where he obtained the degree of Doctor of Medicine. He is the author of numerous popular novels and plays. He died in 1854.

BLAMIRE, SUSANNA . . . . . PAGE 145

    SUSANNA BLAMIRE was a Scotchwoman, born in 1747, who wrote several very clever dialect poems. She died in 1794.

BRENNAN, JOSEPH . . . . . . 322

    JOSEPH BRENNAN was born in the county Donegal, Ireland, on November 17, 1828, but when a child was taken to the city of Cork, where he received a rudimentary education at a private school, and was for a short period at Maynooth College. In 1848 he left Cork for Dublin. His writings there in the *Irish Felon* coming to the notice of government, he was arrested and imprisoned. On his release he edited for a time the *Irishman*. Engaged in a revolutionary attempt in the county Waterford, which failed, he escaped to New York in 1849, where he became connected with the press. In 1851 he removed to New Orleans, where he was a writer for the *Delta* for five years. An attack of yellow fever in 1853 injured his eyes, and he became nearly blind. He came North, and contributed to various journals and magazines. In 1854 he returned to New Orleans. In 1857 he left the *Delta*, and started a daily paper, but died on the 27th of May of the same year, of consumption.

BRETON, NICHOLAS . . . . . . 26

    NICHOLAS BRETON was born in 1555, but in what part of England is unknown. He wrote tales and poems, one volume of these being under the title of "*The Works of a Young Wit.*" He died in 1624.

BROME, ALEXANDER . . . . . . 104

    ALEXANDER BROME was born in London in 1620, and was an attorney of some repute for his satirical powers. He wrote several plays, and a translation of Horace. He died in 1666.

BROOKS, MARIA . . . . . . . 197

    MARIA BROOKS, whose maiden name was Cowen, was born at Medford, in Massachusetts, in 1795. She was married at an early age to Mr. Brooks, a Boston merchant, who left her a widow, at the age of twenty-eight. She then went to reside with a relative in the island of Cuba, where she wrote her poem of "Zophiel," the first canto of which was published in Boston, in 1825. This poem, which is now out of print and almost forgotten, excited at the time no small degree of sensation. Southey, in the *Doctor*, in speaking of its author, styles her "the most impassioned and most imaginative of all poetesses." The poem, under Southey's editorship, was published complete in London, in 1833. She also wrote several minor poems, and a prose romance. She died at Matanzas, November 11, 1845.

WILLIAM BROWNE was born at Tavistock, in Devonshire, in 1590; educated at Exeter College, Oxford; and then entered for the study of law at the Inner Temple. In November, 1624, he was made Master of Arts by Oxford. He is supposed to have died at Otter, in Devonshire, during the winter of 1645.



WILLIAM CULLEN BRYANT was born at Cummington, in Massachusetts, on November 3d, 1794. His earliest productions were translations from the Latin poets, published in the newspaper at Northampton when he was ten years of age; and "The Embargo," a political satire directed at Jefferson, which appeared at Boston in 1808. He entered Williams College at sixteen years of age, but only remained two years, leaving in order to enter on the profession of the law, having been called to the bar in 1815. His poem of "Thanatopsis" appeared in 1816, but was said to have been written three years before. He abandoned the law for literature, and went to New York, where he has since resided. He took editorial charge of the *Evening Post* in 1826, and has maintained his position in that paper up to the present time.



SIR EDWARD LYTTON BULWER-LYTTON, the well-known novelist, was born in Norfolk, England, in 1805, and received his education at Cambridge. He has been long a member of Parliament, and is prominent in the politics of Great Britain. He has published, in poetry, "The New Timon," a not very successful satire; one or two volumes of miscellaneous poems, and several plays, most of which hold possession of the stage.



EDWARD ROBERT BULWER-LYTTON, the son of the novelist, Bulwer-Lytton, was born in 1831. He is in training as a diplomatist and statesman, and usually writes under the name of "Owen Meredith."



WILLIAM H. BURLEIGH was born at Woodstock, Connecticut, on February 2d, 1812, and was taught the art of printing. He soon entered upon editorial duties, and has been connected with a number of journals as editor and contributor. He has also studied law, and is known as a leading "reformer."



ROBERT BURNS was born in Ayrshire, Scotland, on January 25, 1759. From the obscurest station he rose to be the poet of his native land,

and to have a hold on the affections of his people the most enduring.
During his life, however, his abilities brought him no more than a
bare competence.   He died on July 22, 1796.

BYRON, GEORGE GORDON, Baron    .    .    .    PAGE 192

LORD BYRON was born in London, on January 22, 1788, and educated
at Trinity College, Cambridge.   In 1807 he published his juvenile
poems, under the title of "Hours of Idleness."   A sharp and caustic,
but not altogether unjust notice of these, in the *Edinburgh Review*,
excited the anger of the author, and the consequence was "English
Bards and Scotch Reviewers," which appeared in 1809.   He travelled over Europe, and on his return published the first part of "Childe
Harold's Pilgrimage," which at once made him famous.   After the
publication of various and numerous poems, and passing a troubled
and stormy life, he died on April 19, 1824, at Missolonghi, Greece,
whither he had gone to assist the Greeks in their struggle for inde-
pendence.

CAMPBELL, THOMAS    .    .    .    .    .    .    181

THOMAS CAMPBELL was born in Glasgow, Scotland, on July 27, 1777,
and was educated at the University of Glasgow, of which he was afterwards thrice annually elected Lord Rector.   During his life he was
editor of Colburn's *Monthly Magazine*, and also of the *Metropolitan
Magazine*.   He was also the originator of the University of London,
and the author of various prose works, more or less popular.   He died
on the 8th of June, 1844.   His chiefest poem, "The Pleasures of
Hope," was in its time overrated.   It is impossible to overrate some
of his lyrics.   They are, and will probably continue to be, master-
pieces of their kind.

CAREW, THOMAS    .    .    .    .    .    .    .    55

THOMAS CAREW was born—the year is not certain—in Gloucestershire,
and educated at Corpus Christi College, Oxford.   He was made
Gentleman of the Privy Chamber, and Server in Ordinary to King
Charles the First, and died about 1639.

CARTWRIGHT, WILLIAM .    .    .    .    .    .    83

WILLIAM CARTWRIGHT was born at Cirencester, in England, in 1611.
He was ordained, and received, in 1642, an appointment in the
church of Salisbury.   In 1643 he was Junior Proctor, and Reader
in Metaphysics, at Oxford.   He died that year, of malignant fever.
An edition of his "Comedies, tragi-Comedies, and other Poems,"
was published in 1647, and again in 1651.

CHATTERTON, THOMAS    .    .    .    .    .    .    151

THOMAS CHATTERTON was born at Bristol, England, November 20,
1752, and had an imperfect education at Colston's Charity School.

He commenced to write both poetry and prose when a little over eleven years of age.  He was bound apprentice to an attorney, July 1st, 1767.  In 1768, on the occasion of finishing the new bridge at Bristol, there appeared, in Felix Farley's *Bristol Journal*, an account of the ceremonies on opening the old bridge, purporting to be from an ancient MS.  This was traced to Chatterton.  He pretended that this and other manuscripts were found in Mr. Canynge's coffer, an old chest kept over the north porch of Redcliffe church.  From time to time he produced a series of poems, purporting to come from this source, all of which were forgeries.  In 1770 he left the service of Lambert, the attorney, and went to London.  After struggling there in various ways, he committed suicide, August 24, 1770.



HENRY CLAPP, Jr., was born in Newburyport, Massachusetts, in 1814.  With the particulars of his life we are not acquainted.  He has been before the public, as author and lecturer, for many years; and, connected at times with most of the leading journals, and a constant contributor to the abler magazines, he has left a deep mark upon the literature of the country.  He is at present the dramatic critic of a New York weekly of large circulation and strong influence.



HARTLEY COLERIDGE, the eldest son of the famous poet, was born at Clevedon, near Bristol, on September 19, 1796, and was educated at Merton College, Cambridge.  He afterwards became a Fellow of Oriel College.  The Fellowship he forfeited in a year by intemperance.  He went to London, where he became a popular contributor to the various journals and magazines.  He died January 6, 1849.



SAMUEL TAYLOR COLERIDGE was born at Ottery St. Mary, in Devonshire, England, October 21, 1772, and educated at Christ's Hospital, and at Jesus College, Cambridge.  He engaged in literature, travelled for a while in Europe, wrote for the daily press, and published a number of works on various subjects.  He was one of the ten Royal Associates selected at the incorporation of the Royal Society of Literature in 1825.  He died July 25, 1834.



Of HENRY CONSTABLE little is known, except that he was contemporary with Nicholas Breton.  The date of his birth and death cannot be certainly ascertained.



JOHN ESTEN COOKE, the brother of the author of "Florence Vane," was born in Winchester, Frederic county, in Virginia, November 3, 1830.

He was admitted to the bar, and divided his time between law and literature. He is the author of numerous successful novels—the first of which, "Leather Stocking and Silk," appeared in 1853, followed by "The Virginian Comedians" in the following year; "The Youth of Jefferson," "Ellie, or the Human Comedy," "Greenway Court," and "Henry St. John, Gentleman, of the Flower of Hundreds."



PHILIP PENDLETON COOKE was born at the Stone House, Martinsburg, in Virginia, October 26th, 1816, and received his education at Princeton College, New Jersey. He returned to Virginia to live the life of a country gentleman, dabbling in literature as an amusement alone. He wrote both tales and poems, all displaying extraordinary ability; and in 1847 published his "Froissart Ballads." He died in January, 1850.



ABRAHAM COWLEY was born in London in 1618, and educated at Westminster School, and at Cambridge and Oxford. He was appointed Secretary to the Earl of St. Albans, and went with him to the Continent, returning thence in 1656. In 1657 he received the degree of Doctor of Medicine at Oxford. He returned to France on the death of Cromwell, and remained there until the Restoration. He died at the Porch House, Chertsey, in Surrey, in 1667.



RICHARD CRASHAW was educated at Cambridge, where he became a Fellow, but in 1644 he was ejected from his Fellowship by the Earl of Manchester, under authority of Parliament, for refusing to subscribe to the Covenant. He afterwards went abroad, and embraced the Roman Catholic religion. He became Secretary to a Cardinal at Rome, and obtained the office of Canon in the church at Loretto, in 1650, where he shortly afterwards died. His poems were first printed by Thomas Car, in 1646, during Crashaw's exile.



ALLAN CUNNINGHAM was born at Blackwood, on Nithside, December 7th, 1784. He was taken from school at eleven years of age, to be made a mason, and became a good workman; but his literary taste led him to London in 1810, where, in 1814, he became superintendent of the sculptor Chantrey's studio. He wrote several works that survive. He died in 1842.



SAMUEL DANYELL, the son of a teacher of music, was born near Taunton, in Somersetshire, in 1562, and received his education at Magdalen Hall, Oxford. He was patronized by the Countess of Pembroke, and others of the nobility, particularly the Earl of Southampton; and had the manliness to address a laudatory poem to the latter upon his downfall. He was made Gentleman Extraordinary to King James, and afterwards Groom of the Privy Chamber to the Queen. He died on his farm at Beckington, in Somersetshire, in October, 1619. His wife was Justina, the sister of John Florio, the author of an Italian Dictionary celebrated in its day.

DAVENANT, SIR WILLIAM . . . . PAGE 81

SIR WILLIAM DAVENANT, the son of a vintner, who kept the Crown Inn at Oxford, was born in the latter part of February, 1605–6. He was educated partly at Lincoln College, Oxford, but took no degree. Early in life he became a page of the Duchess of Richmond, but losing this place, turned his attention to literature, and became a successful dramatist. This secured him the patronage and influence of the Earl of Dorset and others, and he succeeded Jonson as Poet Laureate, in 1638. Accused to the Parliament of endeavoring to weaken its authority over the army, he was arrested, and, though bailed, was obliged to leave for France. He returned, and was appointed Lieutenant-general of Ordnance to the Marquis of Newcastle; and for his conduct at the siege of Gloucester, in 1643, was knighted by the King. He went into exile in France before the failure of the Royal cause. In 1650, at the instance of the Queen, he set sail for Virginia, but was taken by a Parliamentary ship, and sent prisoner to the Isle of Wight. From thence he was removed to the Tower, but his life was saved by powerful private interposition—some say by John Milton. If so, he returned the favor, for it was owing to his influence that Milton was saved at the Restoration. On the return of the King, Davenant devoted himself principally to dramatic affairs. He died at Lincoln's-Inn-Fields, on April 7th, 1668.

DAVIS, THOMAS OSBORNE . . . . . 289

THOMAS OSBORNE DAVIS was born at Mallow, in the county of Cork, Ireland, in the year 1814, and was educated at Trinity College, Dublin. It was not until he was nearly thirty years of age that he appeared as a poet. The political events of the day, and the necessity of national poetry in the *Nation*, the journal under his editorial care, brought forth a series of poems, filled with fire, pathos, and energy, though without the perfect skill of the artist. He died September 16, 1845.

DAWES, RUFUS . . . . . . . 242

RUFUS DAWES was born in Boston, January 26, 1803; and after a partial education at Harvard College, entered upon the study of the law, and was admitted to the bar. He has, however, made literature, to a certain extent, his profession—certainly his pursuit. He died Nov. 30th, 1859.

DERMODY, THOMAS . . . . . . 175

THOMAS DERMODY was born at Ennis, in the county Clare, Ireland, in 1774. He went to Dublin when a boy, and entered the service of a bookseller. While there, his writings attracted the attention of persons of condition, and he was patronized by the Countess of Moira, who placed him under the tuition of the Rev. Hugh Boyd. At the age of fifteen he produced a volume of poems, which were promising. But he grew precociously dissipated and reckless, and was soon abandoned by his new friends. He died July 15, 1802, at Sydenham Common, and was buried at Lewisham, where Sir James Bland Burgess gave him a monument.



CHARLES DIBDIN was born at Southampton, England, in 1745, and appeared as an actor in 1762, firstly in the provinces, and afterwards at London. He wrote successful plays, and over twelve hundred songs, to most of which he set the music. He died in 1814.



THOMAS DIBDIN, son of Charles, the sailor bard, was born in London, in 1771. He was apprenticed to an upholsterer from his sixteenth to his twentieth year. He then joined a troop of strolling players; and afterwards wrote successfully for the stage during many years. Some of his pieces are still occasionally played. He died on September 16th, 1841.



ANNE P. SHACKLEFORD was born at Charleston, South Carolina, in 1810. In 1830 she was married to John C. Dinnies, of St. Louis. She has published a collection of her poems, under the title of "The Floral Year."



JOHN DONNE, the son of an eminent merchant of Welsh descent, was born in London, in 1573, and was educated partly at Oxford, and partly at Trinity College, Cambridge. He was with the Earl of Essex in his expedition against Cadiz; and travelled for some years in the south of Europe. On his return to England he was made Secretary to Sir Thomas Egerton, Lord Keeper of the Great Seal. He made a stolen match, in 1602, with Anna, daughter of Sir George Moore, Chancellor of the Garter. This involved the loss of his position, imprisonment, and a tedious and ruinous lawsuit. By the interposition of powerful friends, a reconciliation between himself and his father-in-law was finally effected. He was afterwards made a Master of Arts by both Oxford and Cambridge. About 1611 he entered into holy orders, and filled various clerical positions respectably. He died on March 31st, 1631, of consumption. His poems were first printed complete in one volume by Tonson, 1719.



CHARLES SACKVILLE, LORD BUCKHURST, was born January 24, 1637, and educated privately. He was chosen member of Parliament for East

Grinsted, immediately after the Restoration, and became one of the favorites of Charles the Second. In 1665, he was at sea during the sea-fight wherein the Dutch admiral, Opdam, was blown up, and thirty ships of the enemy taken and destroyed. It was just previous to this engagement that his celebrated song, "To all you Ladies," is said to have been composed. He was then made Gentleman of the Bedchamber; and, in 1675, created Earl of Middlesex, having previously inherited the former Earl's fortune. In 1667, on the death of his father, he became Earl of Dorset. He opposed the course of James the Second, and voted for an acknowledgment of the claims of the Prince and Princess of Orange. He became a favorite with William the Third, who made him Lord Chamberlain of the Household, and, in 1691, Knight of the Garter. During the absence of the King, he was four times placed on the Regency. He died January 19th, 1705–6.



DR. DRAKE was born in New York, on August 7th, 1795. He received his education at Columbia College, and chose the practice of medicine as a profession. He died of consumption, in September, 1820. He gave great promise, not so much in his "Culprit Fay," or "American Flag," his popular efforts, as in other minor pieces, which displayed pathos, tenderness, and force, in a great degree.



MICHAEL DRAYTON was born at Atherston, in Leicestershire about 1563. He was the son of a respectable butcher. Though a student for a time at Oxford, it is thought that he completed his education at Cambridge, under the patronage of Henry Goodere, and others. He was one of the esquires attending Sir Walter Aston, when the latter was created Knight of the Bath, but does not seem to have attained court preferment. He died in 1631. His "Poly-Olbion" is a singular and remarkable production. His "Nymphidia" is considered by many to be masterly throughout. His "Ballad of Agincourt" is exceedingly spirited.



WILLIAM DRUMMOND was born at Hawthornden, Mid-Lothian, on December 13th, 1585. He was the son of Sir John Drummond, and was educated at the University of Edinburgh, where he received the degree of Master of Arts. He studied the civil law at Bruges, in France, and in 1611 returned to Scotland. He soon abandoned the profession of law for the charms of the Muses. Losing the lady of his love by death, a short while before the day fixed for their marriage, he at once went abroad again, and travelled over Europe during eight years. In 1630 he married Elizabeth Logan, in whom he saw a resemblance to his first love, to whose memory he had remained faithful. He died December 4th, 1649. In addition to his Poems, he wrote a History of the Five Jameses, folio, first printed in London, in 1655. His complete works were first published at Edinburgh, by Watson, in 1711.

DRYDEN, JOHN . . . . . . . PAGE 108

John Dryden was born on the 9th of August, 1631, at Aldwinckle, in Northamptonshire, England, and educated firstly at Westminster, and then at Cambridge. He entered upon his literary career early, and soon became involved in politics, wherein his course was erratic and censurable. His works are numerous, and he is considered as one of the greatest of English poets. He died on May 1st, 1700, and was buried in Westminster Abbey, where a monument was erected to his memory by the Duke of Buckingham.

EMBURY, EMMA C. . . . . . . 268

Emma C. Manley was born in New York, in 1807, and is the wife of Mr. Daniel Embury, of Brooklyn. She has published several volumes of poems.

EMERSON, RALPH WALDO . . . . . 244

Ralph W. Emerson was born in Boston, Massachusetts, in 1803, and educated at Harvard College. In 1829 he was ordained, but abandoned the pulpit, in consequence of a change of religious views. He is known better as a writer of the "Dial" school, which he leads, than as a poet.

ENGLAND, ELIZABETH TUDOR, QUEEN OF . . . 17

Elizabeth Tudor, afterwards famous as "the Virgin Queen," was born September 7, 1533, and ascended the throne in 1558. She was able, brilliant, vain, and cruel; advancing the power of the realm, and administering public affairs with credit and success. She died March 24, 1603.

ENGLISH, THOMAS DUNN . . . . . 302

Thomas Dunn English was born at Philadelphia, on June 29th, 1819. He received the degree of Doctor of Medicine from the University of Pennsylvania in 1839, and was called to the bar in 1842. He has written novels, poems, plays, and miscellaneous works. His ballad "Ben Bolt," and his Revolutionary Ballads, most of which last were published in *Harper's Magazine*, are best known. He has also mingled in politics, but has held no official position, with the exception of having served two terms recently in the New Jersey Legislature. He is connected with two New York journals, as editor.

ETHEREGE, SIR GEORGE . . . . . . 111

Sir George Etherege was born near London, about 1636, and educated

at Cambridge. He travelled awhile in Europe, and studied law, but
forsook that profession for literature. In 1664 he published a successful comedy—"The Comical Revenge, or Love in a Tub;" in 1668,
"She Would if She Could;" and in 1676, "The Man of Mode."
He died after 1688, but the exact year is uncertain.



GILES FLETCHER was born about 1588. He was the younger brother of
Phineas Fletcher, the author of "The Purple Island," the son of Giles
Fletcher, author of "The Russe Commonwealth," and cousin of John
Fletcher, the dramatist. He was educated at Trinity College, Cam-
bridge, and took orders. He was incumbent for a while of the living
of Alderton, in Suffolk, where he died in 1623.



JOHN FLETCHER, the coadjutor of Beaumont, was born in Northamptonshire, England, in 1576, and educated at Cambridge. He died of the
plague, in 1625.



This GRAHAM was a Scotchman, who was born in 1735, and died in
1797. Beyond this, little is known of him.



ROBERT GREENE was born at Norwich, in 1560 (but some writers fix
the date ten years previously), and was educated at St. John's College,
Cambridge. He travelled on the Continent; and after his return, in
1583, received the degree of Master of Arts from Cambridge. He
wrote stories, treatises, and poems, attaining fair success in each depart-
ment of literature. He died on September 3d, 1592.



EDMUND DORR GRIFFIN was born in Wyoming, Pennsylvania, September
10th, 1804, and was educated at Columbia College, New York. He
was ordained deacon in 1826; travelled in Europe from 1828 to 1830,
when, on returning, he was appointed to a professorship in Columbia
College, which he soon resigned on account of his ill health. He died
on September 1st, 1830.



WILLIAM HABINGTON, who is called by Wood "a very accomplished
gentleman," was born at Hendlip, in Worcestershire, in 1605, and
educated at St. Omers and Paris. He died on November 30th, 1654.



FITZ-GREENE HALLECK was born at Guilford, in Connecticut, in August,
1795; but removed, when eighteen years old, to New York, which

has since been his residence. His lyrics, "Marco Bozzaris," "Burns,"
and "Red Jacket," are well known, and on these mainly his pretensions
rest. His works were first published in 1827, a more complete edition
in 1836, and another in 1847.



JOHN HARRINGTON was born in 1534, but in what part of England is unknown. He was imprisoned in the Tower on account of a correspond-
ence with the Princess Elizabeth, who rewarded him for his fidelity, on
her accession to the throne. He died in 1582.



PAUL H. HAYNE was born in Charleston, South Carolina, in 1831. He
has been for some time connected with the press, and has contributed
to several of the magazines. His collected works were published in
1855.



ROBERT HERRICK was born at Cheapside, London, in 1591, and educated
at Cambridge. He took orders, and became Vicar of Dean Prior, in
Devonshire. He lost his living by the civil war, but regained it on
the Restoration. He was probably near eighty when he died, but the
year of his death is not fixed.



Little is known of HEYWOOD, except that he was a good linguist, and
wrote 220 plays, of which twenty-four are now extant. He wrote
from 1596 to 1640, and probably died during the latter year, or the
year after.



AARON HILL was born in the Strand, London, on February 10th, 1684–5.
When a boy he went on a visit to his relative, Lord Paget, then Ambassador at Constantinople. The latter gave the young adventurer a
tutor; and after travelling with him over Europe, brought him home
in 1713. Young Hill travelled afterwards as a tutor in Europe; and
returning home, became the manager of a theatre, wrote several successful plays, and engaged in various speculations, mostly unsuccessful.
He died February 8th, 1749–50. He was a voluminous writer, and
by some of his cotemporaries was placed above Pope. His writings
are now as unjustly obscure, as they were formerly undeservedly pre-
eminent.



CHARLES FENNO HOFFMAN was born in New York, in 1806, and was
educated at Columbia College, New York, where he received a Master's degree. He was admitted to the bar three years after leaving

college, but abandoned law for literature. He was the author of
several popular novels; and a complete collection of his poems was
published in 1845.

HOLMES, OLIVER WENDELL    .    .    .    .    PAGE 278

OLIVER WENDELL HOLMES was born August 29th, 1809, at Cambridge,
Massachusetts, and was educated at Harvard College. He received
the degree of Doctor of Medicine in 1836. In 1838 he was made
Professor of Anatomy and Physiology at Dartmouth Medical College;
and in 1847, Parkman Professor of Anatomy and Physiology at Harvard. In addition to his poems, he has published successful books of
essays, and several medical works. He is one of the constant contrib
utors to the *Atlantic Monthly*.

HUNTER, ANNE    .    .    .    .    .    .    .    139

ANNE HOME, who was a sister of Sir Everard Home, was born in 1742,
and was known in her day as the author of several clever poems. She
married the celebrated surgeon, Hunter. She died in London, in 1821.

IDE, A. M.    .    .    .    .    .    .    .    .    312

MR. IDE is the editor of the *Taunton Gazette*, and was born in Massachusetts, in 1825. He has written poems for various periodicals, and
managed his journal with ability. He was at one time postmaster
of his town.

JONSON, BEN .    .    .    .    .    .    .    .    53

BEN JONSON ("O rare Ben Jonson!" as his tombstone has it) was born in
Warwickshire, on June 11th, 1574. After receiving a partial education at the College School of Westminster, he was removed by his
stepfather, and made to work at the latter's trade, which was that of
a bricklayer. He ultimately entered at Cambridge, where he did not
long remain, but became an actor and writer of plays. He served also
for a while as a soldier in the Low Countries. In 1598, the success
of "Every Man in his Humour" decided his career. In 1619, Oxford
made him a Master of Arts; and on the death of Danyell, he was
created Poet Laureate. He died in London, on August 6th, 1637.
His works are voluminous.

KEATS, JOHN    .    .    .    .    .    .    .    207

JOHN KEATS was born at Moorfields, London, in 1796, and was apprenticed to a surgeon, at an early age. Evincing literary talent, he was
introduced, by the gentleman who had been his schoolmaster, to Leigh
Hunt, who brought him before the public. A volume of his poems
was issued in 1817, and after this "Endymion" appeared. The savage
attack upon this by the *Quarterly Review* was said to have brought on
his death; but this was an error. He published a third volume afterwards, containing some clever effusions. He died at Rome, whither he
had gone on account of ill health, on February 24th, 1821.

HENRY KING was born in 1591, and was educated at Christ Church College, Oxford, where he took his degree of A. M. He was appointed Chaplain to James the First, and in 1638 was made Dean of Rochester. In 1641 he was created Bishop of Chichester. He died in 1669. He was author of several volumes of Sermons, a Poetic Version of the Psalms, and a volume of Poems.



JOHN LAPRAIK'S time of birth is not certain, but it was somewhere between 1738 and 1742. He met with misfortunes by the failure of the Ayr Bank, which forced him to sell his property near Muirkirk. It was during this time of trouble that he composed his song, "Matrimonial Happiness." Lapraik was the friend and correspondent of Burns, and died in 1807.



JAMES LAWSON was born November 9, 1799, in Glasgow, Scotland, and educated at the University of his native city. He came to this country in 1815, and entered his uncle's counting-house. He was successful for a time as a merchant, but the failure of the house with which he was connected drove him into literature as a profession. He was for many years connected with the press of New York, and was a frequent contributor to the leading magazines.



WILLIAM LEGGETT was born in New York, in the summer of 1802, and was educated at Georgetown College. He entered the navy in 1822, but retired from the service in 1826, and assumed the profession of letters. He wrote poems, tales, and sketches, all with more than average ability, and finally became associated with Bryant in the management of the *Evening Post*. This he left for a journal of his own, *The Plaindealer*, which attained reputation, but was not profitable. He was appointed a diplomatic agent to Guatemala, in 1840, but died before he could set out on his mission, on May 29th of the same year.



JOHN LEYDEN was born at Denholm, in Roxburghshire, Scotland, on September 8th, 1775, and educated at the University of Edinburgh. He took orders in the Presbyterian Church, but failed as a preacher. He then commenced the study of medicine, and was made an assistant-surgeon in the East India Company's service, in 1802. While in India he was promoted to the grade of surgeon; then made Professor of Hindustani in Fort William College; next, the Judge of the Twenty-four Pargunnahs of Calcutta; and, in 1810, was appointed Assay-master of the Calcutta Mint. He accompanied Lord Minto in his expedition against Java, and died there, August 28th, 1816.

The year of LODGE's birth, set down as 1556, is not certainly known, but he was educated at Trinity College, Oxford, where he became servitor in 1573. He was a student at law at Lincoln's Inn in 1584, then became an actor, and at length, after studying medicine on the Continent, took his Doctor's degree at Avignon. He wrote various novels, plays, and miscellaneous productions, and died in 1625, at London, of the plague, while engaged in the practice of medicine.



JOHN LOGAN was born at Soutra, in Mid-Lothian, Scotland, about 1748, and was educated at the University of Edinburgh. He was private tutor to Mr., afterward Sir John Sinclair. His tragedy of " Runnimede," refused license by the Chamberlain, was brought out in Edinburgh in 1784. He was ordained minister of South Leith in 1773, but left that position in 1786, and went to London. He died December 28th, 1788.



HENRY WADSWORTH LONGFELLOW was born at Portland, Maine, February 27th, 1807, and was educated at Bowdoin College. He was made Professor of Modern Languages in Bowdoin, in 1826, and travelled over Europe for nearly four years, to fit himself for his professorship. In 1835 he succeeded Mr. Ticknor as Professor of Modern Languages and Literature in Harvard College, which he held for a number of years. After a few years he resigned, and was succeeded by Lowell. Besides poems, he has written novels, travels, and reviews, and attained a high reputation as the head of the American poets.



RICHARD LOVELACE was born at Walbridge, in Kent, England, in 1618, and educated at Oxford. He was imprisoned and banished for his attachment to the Royal cause; and, while absent, commanded a regiment in the French army. In this service he was wounded, and returned to England, where he was imprisoned again, but at length released. During his absence, the lady to whom he addressed his love poems—his " Lucasta" and " Althea,"—believing him to have been killed, married another. He died in London, in want, during 1658.



JAMES RUSSELL LOWELL was born at Boston, in 1819, was educated at Harvard College, and afterwards admitted to the bar. He is at present a Professor at Cambridge, Massachusetts, and is a constant contributor to the *Atlantic Monthly.*



JOHN LYLYE was born in Kent, England, during 1553, and educated at

Magdalen College, Oxford, where he took his Master's degree, in 1575. He was the author of the celebrated " Euphues, or Anatomy of Wit," and of several plays, and died about 1600.



GEORGE LYTTELTON was born in Worcestershire, England, January 17, 1708-9, and educated at Christ Church College, Oxford. He travelled for a time in Europe, and on his return became a member of Parliament. In 1744 he was made one of the Lords of the Treasury; in 1754, Cofferer to the Household, and Privy Councillor; and in 1755, Chancellor of the Exchequer. In 1757 he was created Baron Lyttelton, of Frankley. He died August 22d, 1773.



HECTOR M'Neill, was born at Rosebank, near Roslin, Scotland, in 1746. He went, when a young man, to St. Christopher, and there entered on a mercantile life, with good prospects; but an act of imprudence cost him his situation, and he became much reduced in circumstances. He returned to Scotland at the age of forty. He now used his literary abilities to eke out a subsistence, though but a scanty one; publishing several volumes, one of these a novel of moderate merit, and two of them poems—" Scotland's Skaith," and " The Waes o' Man"—that have retained provincial distinction. He also edited for a time the *Scots Magazine*. He died on March 15th, 1818.



DAVID MALLET was born about 1700, and is supposed to have been a native of Perthshire, Scotland. He was educated at the University of Edinburgh, and became tutor to the sons of the Duke of Montrose. He was at one time Secretary to the Prince of Wales. He wrote various plays, which were produced between 1731 and 1763 in London, some successfully, and others not. In 1763 he was made Keeper of the Book of Entries for Ships in the Port of London. He died in April, 1765.



CHRISTOPHER MARLOWE was born at Canterbury, in Kent, during 1562, and educated at Bennet College, Cambridge, where he was made Master of Arts in 1587. He wrote tragedies and plays, and became an actor, but left the stage, after having broken his leg. He was slain in a street brawl, at Deptford, in May, 1593.



ANDREW MARVEL was born at Hull, England, during 1620, and probably educated under the supervision of his father, who was Master of the Grammar School there. He was a vigorous and effective satirist during the days of the Commonwealth, and a strong opponent of the Court party. He died in 1678.

WILLIAM JULIUS MICKLE was born at Langholm, Dumfriesshire, September 29th, 1734. His translation of the "Lusiad" of Camoens appeared in 1775. In 1780 he was made a member of the Royal Academy of Lisbon. He was Secretary to Commodore Johnston, in command of the *Romney*, and afterwards appointed joint agent for the prizes taken. He thus acquired a competence, married, and settled at Wheatley, near Oxford, where he died, October 25th, 1789.



JAMES GRAHAM, of Montrose, was born in Scotland, in 1612, and succeeded his father, as fifth Earl, when he was but fourteen. He was married soon after, and travelled abroad until 1633. He took ground at first with those who opposed the Church party in Scotland, and was a leading actor in the preparation of the National Covenant. He afterwards went over to the King's party, and was arrested and imprisoned; but upon the occasion of some concessions made by Charles, in 1642, he was released. In 1644 he was created Marquis, and made Captain-General, and Commander-in-chief for Scotland. In this capacity he won a series of battles, and was successful until he met with Lesley, who defeated him at Philiphaugh, September 13th, 1645. On the King's surrender he capitulated, and was permitted to escape to Norway, which he did on September 3d, 1646. He was offered the posts of General of Scots in France, Lieutenant-general in the French army, and Captain of Gens d'armes, but refused. On the death of Charles the First, his son commissioned Montrose to invade Scotland. The Marquis dispatched some of his troops here in September, 1649, and joined them in the following March. In the first battle his forces were routed, and himself captured. He was treated with great indignity, and on May 21st, 1650, was hanged on a gibbet thirty feet high, and his body afterwards quartered. He received his fate with such firmness and dignity as to excite even the pity of his enemies.



THOMAS MOORE was born in Dublin, on May 28th, 1780, and educated at Trinity College, Dublin. In 1803 he was made Registrar to the Admiralty, at Bermuda; but the place not suiting his inclinations, he returned to England in 1804. He has written two plays, with questionable success, and several miscellaneous works, but his reputation depends upon his poems. He died on February 25th, 1852.



GEORGE P. MORRIS was born in Philadelphia, in the year 1801. He commenced his literary career at an early age; and in 1823, in connection with Woodworth, established the *New York Mirror*. He was for a long while connected with Willis in the publication of the *Home*

*Journal.* He has written several successful plays, and divers popular tales, but is better known as a song-writer. His " Woodman, spare that Tree!" is one of the few popular American songs. He died in 1864.

MOTHERWELL, WILLIAM . . . . . PAGE 218

WILLIAM MOTHERWELL was born at Glasgow, Scotland, on October 13th, 1797. He published several successful volumes, wrote spirited ballads, edited two or three provincial magazines, and attained great distinction as an antiquary. He died on November 1st, 1835.

NORTON, CAROLINE ELIZABETH SARAH . . . 274

MRS. NORTON is a granddaughter of Richard Brinsley Sheridan, and second daughter of Thomas Sheridan, and was born in London, in what year we are not informed. She married with the Hon. G. C. Norton, a brother of Lord Grantley, but the union has proved unhappy.

OSGOOD, FRANCES S. . . . . . . 286

FRANCES S. LOCKE was born in Boston, Massachusetts, in 1812, and commenced to write at an early age. In 1834 she was married to Mr. S. S. Osgood, the artist. She published various volumes of her poems from time to time, all of which had fair success. She died in New York, on May 12th, 1850.

OXFORD EDWARD VERE, EARL OF . . . . 19

EDWARD VERE, Earl of Oxford, was born in 1562. He was one of the favourites at the court of Elizabeth, married a daughter of Lord Burleigh, was connected with Leicester's expedition to the Netherlands, and took part in the defeat of the Spanish Armada. He wrote a number of comedies that were highly praised by cotemporary critics, but none of these are extant. He died in 1604.

PATTISON, WILLIAM . . . . . . 126

WILLIAM PATTISON was born at Peasmarsh, near Rye, in the county of Sussex, England, in 1706. He was educated partially at Sidney College, Cambridge. He died, in great distress, July 11th, 1727.

PERCY, THOMAS . . . . . . . 133

BISHOP PERCY was born at Bridgenorth, in Shropshire, England, in 1728, and educated at Christ Church College, Oxford. He received the degree of Master of Arts in 1753, and was appointed Chaplain to the King. In 1778 he was made Dean of Carlisle; and in 1782, Bishop of Dromore, in Ireland. He died during 1811.

PINKNEY, EDWARD COATE . . . . . 227

EDWARD COATE PINKNEY, the son of a former American minister to England, was born in London, at the Embassy, in October, 1802. He

received a partial education at the College of St. Mary's, Baltimore,
and then entered the Navy as a midshipman. He continued in the
service nine years, but resigned his position on the death of his father.
In 1824 he was admitted to the bar. In the profession of law he
failed, and also failed in an attempt to enter the naval service of
Mexico. In 1826 he was appointed a Professor in the University of
Maryland; but his constitution was broken, and after lingering through
a weary year or two, he died, April 11th, 1828.


EDGAR ALLAN POE was born in Baltimore, Maryland, in January, 1811.
He was partially educated at a school in England, and partly at the
University of Virginia, but never completed his education. He was
for a short period a cadet at West Point, went abroad for a year on a
Quixotic expedition, and for a time was a private soldier in the Army,
but he deserted before his time of service expired. He passed a varied,
but miserable life, and died of delirium tremens, in a hospital in Baltimore, on October 7th, 1849.


GEORGE D. PRENTICE was born at Preston, in Connecticut, in the year
1804, and was educated at Brown University, Providence. He has
been for many years the editor of the *Louisville Journal*, in Kentucky.


BRYAN WALLER PROCTOR, better known as "Barry Cornwall," was born
in London, about 1796. He was educated at Harrow, and is a barris-
ter, enjoying a fair practice. He is, or was, Commissioner of Lunacy.


MATTHEW PRIOR was born at Winborne, in Dorsetshire, England, July
21st, 1664, and educated at St. John's College, Cambridge. In 1691
he was made Secretary to the Earl of Berkeley, Ambassador and Pleni-
potentiary at the Congress of the Hague, and afterwards Gentleman of
the Bedchamber. In 1697, he was Secretary to the English Plenipo-
tentiary at the treaty of Ryswick, and the same year was made Secretary to the Lord Lieutenant of Ireland. In 1698 he was Secretary
of Legation at Paris, and filled afterwards other diplomatic and official
positions. In 1700 he was made Master of Arts by mandamus. He
was member of Parliament in 1701. In August, 1713, he was appointed Ambassador to Paris, and on his return to England was arrested,
March 25th, 1715, by order of the House of Commons, on a charge
of high treason. In 1717, he was specially excepted from the act of
grace passed by Parliament; but was finally discharged, a ruined man.
He died September 18th, 1721.

RALEIGH, SIR WALTER . . . . . PAGE 21

WALTER RALEIGH was born at Hayes, in Devonshire, England, during
1552, and educated at Oriel College, Oxford. His life was a succes-
sion of achievements, explorations, intrigues, and troubles. In 1569,
he went to France with an expedition in aid of the Huguenots, served
there for five years, and subsequently in the Netherlands, under the
Prince of Orange. He next went with Sir Humphrey Gilbert on a
voyage to America, from whence he returned in 1579. In 1580, he
commanded a company of the royal troops in Ireland, against the Earl
of Desmond. Three years afterwards he was introduced at court,
where he became a favourite of Elizabeth. He was knighted, made
Captain of the Guard, Seneschal of the county of Cornwall, and Lord
Warden of the Stannaries, with a grant of 12,000 acres from the
forfeited estates of the Earl of Desmond, and a patent for licensing
the vendors of wine in England. In 1584, he obtained a patent au-
thorizing to hold forever any territories he might acquire in America.
In 1585 he landed in Virginia. From this voyage tobacco was first
brought, and the potato plant introduced into England. From this
time forth he was engaged in many stormy adventures; but having
lost the favor of James the First, he was convicted of high treason,
and, it is generally thought, unjustly, in 1603. He was reprieved, and
remained a close prisoner in the Tower for thirteen years. In 1615,
he was released conditionally, to open a mine in Guiana. On this
voyage he had an encounter with the Spaniards, was unsuccessful in
finding the mine, and, his crew mutinying, was obliged to return to
England. Here the brutal pedant, King James, caused him to be
executed under the old sentence, on October 28th, 1618.


ROCHESTER, JOHN WILMOT, EARL OF . . . 119

JOHN WILMOT, Earl of Rochester, was born at Ditchley, near Woodstock,
in Oxfordshire, England, on April 10th, 1647, and was educated at
Oxford, where he was made Master of Arts, in 1661. He travelled
in France and Italy, and on his return was made Gentleman of the
Bedchamber to Charles the Second, and Comptroller of Woodstock
Park. In 1665 he went to sea with the Earl of Sandwich, and distinguished himself in that and the following year. He was witty,
profligate, and abandoned. He died July 26th, 1680.


ROCKWELL, JAMES OTIS . . . . . . 257

JAMES OTIS ROCKWELL was born at Lebanon, Connecticut, in 1807. He
was taught the art of a printer, and became editor of the *Boston Statesman*. In 1820, he became editor and publisher of the *Providence
Patriot*. In this last position he died, during the summer of 1831.
His poems have never been collected.

32*

General Eaton at Tunis; went with Lord Selkirk to Lake St. Clair, where the latter desired to found a colony; and after wandering for some time, settled at Annapolis, and commenced the practice of his profession. In 1807, he married and removed to Baltimore. He died January 10th, 1809.



PERCY BYSSHE SHELLEY was born at Horsham, in Sussex, England, on August 4th, 1792, and educated at University College, Oxford. He wrote several atheistical and other works, and some of the most highly imaginative poems in the language. He was drowned off Leghorn, Italy, July 8th, 1821.



NATHANIEL G. SHEPHERD was born in New York, in 1836; and is known as a contributor, in both prose and poetry, to various leading journals.



RICHARD BRINSLEY SHERIDAN was born at Dublin, Ireland, in September, 1751, and educated at Trinity College, Dublin. He wrote some of the most celebrated comedies, farces, operas, and dramas in the language, all of which yet hold possession of the stage. He also shone as a politician, and was elected in 1780 to Parliament, where he further distinguished himself. He was for a time one of the proprietors of Drury Lane Theatre, from which, on his second marriage, in 1795, he retired to a small estate in Surrey. There he remained until 1798, when he returned to London to bring out two of his plays, translations and amplifications from Kotzebue—"The Stranger," and "Pizarro." He died on July 7th, 1816.



SIR PHILIP SIDNEY was born at Penshurst, in Kent, England, on November 29th, 1554, and educated at Christ Church, Oxford. He travelled in Europe from 1572 to 1575. In 1576 he was Special Ambassador to the court of Vienna. It is asserted that in 1585 he was offered, and declined, the crown of Poland. That year he was made Governor of Flushing. He was killed in battle at Zutphen, in the Low Countries, September 22d, 1586. He wrote a series of poems, and numerous other works, including "Arcadia," and the "Defence of Poesie."



JOHN SKELTON was born in Cumberland, England, about 1463, and educated at Oxford, where he took the laurel crown for poetry, in 1489. He took orders, and became Rector of Dysse, in Norfolk; but was finally suspended on account of the immoral tendency of his writings. He died on June 21st, 1529.

SIR JOHN SUCKLING was born at Witham, in Middlesex, in 1613. He is said to have spoken Latin at five years of age, and to have written it at nine—which is almost too absurd to be repeated. One of his biographers says, quite innocently—"If this circumstance be true, it would seem that he had learned Latin from his nurse, nor ever heard any other language, for it is not to be supposed that he could speak Latin at five in consequence of study." He became Comptroller of the Household to Charles the First. When the civil war broke out, he raised and headed a troop of horse, at a great expense; but neither he nor his troop did much nor effective service. He died on March 7th, 1641, of a fever. His productions are notable, though marked with the coarseness and sensuality of the time; and among them, his "Ballad on a Wedding" is justly celebrated.



The EARL OF SURREY was the son of the Duke of Norfolk, Lord Treasurer of England, and the grandson of another duke who had held the same position. He received an excellent education at Cardinal Wolsey's College, at Oxford, and was among the foremost wits and gallants of his time. It is said of him, that the celebrated Cornelius Agrippa, with whom he had an acquaintance, showed him, in his celebrated magic glass, his love, Geraldine, reclining on a couch, sick, and reading by a wax taper one of her lover's sonnets. The Earl served in the Army, distinguishing himself at the battle of Flodden; but afterwards failed, in the expedition to Boulogne, where he held the position of field-marshal. This failure ended his military career, and lost him the favour of King Henry. He was finally tried, and convicted of high treason, though on the most frivolous grounds, and was beheaded on Tower-Hill, on January 19th, 1546-7. His "Geraldine" was Lady Elizabeth Fitzgerald, second daughter of Gerald Fitzgerald, Earl of Kildare, and afterwards third wife of Edward Clinton, Earl of Lincoln. His "Songes and Sonnettes" were first collected along with those of Sir Thomas Wyat, the elder, and others, and published by Tottell, in London, 1557.



JOSHUA SYLVESTER was born in 1563. He was a merchant, but became known to Queen Elizabeth through his wit, and was a favourite with her and her successor. From some cause not clearly stated, he was obliged to leave England during the reign of James the First, and died in Holland, September 28th, 1618.



ROBERT TANNAHILL was born June 3d, 1774, at Paisley, Scotland, where he worked at the trade of a weaver. He died May 17th, 1810.

JAMES BAYARD TAYLOR was born January 11th, 1825, at Kennet Square, Chester county, Pennsylvania. He left for Europe in 1844, and travelled a-foot over the Continent. Since that time he has travelled over half the globe, and published several popular volumes of travels. His reputation will rest more on his poetry, however, than his prose.



ALFRED TENNYSON was born at Somerset, in Lincolnshire, England, in 1810, and educated at Trinity College, Cambridge. He was made Poet Laureate on the death of Wordsworth, and Oxford has given him the degree of Doctor of the Civil Law. He is known alone by his poems, of which he has published several volumes; and may be said to have founded a new school of poetry.



FREDERICK W. THOMAS was born at Providence, Rhode Island, October 25th, 1808. He was admitted to the bar, at an early age, at Charleston, South Carolina, where he had resided from his childhood, and in 1834 he removed to Cincinnati. He has written several successful novels and historical works.



JAMES THOMSON was born at Ednam, near Kelso, in Roxburghshire, Scotland, September 11th, 1700, and was educated partly at a school in Jedburgh, and partly at the University of Edinburgh. He published his "Winter," in 1726, in London, where its reception was highly favourable. Between that and 1730, the remainder of the poems making up "The Seasons" were published. He failed in tragedy—his "Sophonisba" meeting with bad success at Drury Lane. He travelled in Europe as tutor to the Hon. Charles Talbot, son of the Chancellor, and on his return was made Secretary of the Briefs. A posthumous tragedy, called "Coriolanus," was produced in 1749. He died August 27th, 1748.



AUBREY THOMAS DE VERE is the third son of Sir Aubrey de Vere, the author of "Julian the Apostate," and other works, and was born January 10th, 1814. He has published two different volumes of poetry. The family were originally Irish, and named Hunt; but the father of our poet assumed the arms and surname of De Vere in 1832, by letters-patent.



WILLIAM ROSS WALLACE was born in Kentucky, in 1818, and educated, we believe, at an Indiana College. He has been admitted to the bar, but is a literary man by profession. Some of his lyrics are exceedingly noble, and will live.



EDMUND WALLER was born at Coleshill, in Hertfordshire, England, March 3d, 1605, and educated at Eton, and King's College, Cambridge. He was chosen member of Parliament at eighteen years of age, and banished in 1643, for being engaged in a plot for the king's restoration, but was at length permitted to return. He served in Parliament during the reigns of Charles the Second and James the Second, being elected to the first Parliament of the latter sovereign when in his eightieth year. He died October 21st, 1687. He enjoyed successively the favor of James I., Charles I., Cromwell, Charles II., and James II.



WILLIAM WALSH, the correspondent and friend of Pope, was born at Abberley, in Worcestershire, England, in 1663, and educated at Oxford. He sat several times in Parliament.



JOHN GREENLEAF WHITTIER was born at Haverhill, Massachusetts, in 1808. He commenced writing for the journals at an early age, and at twenty-one became an editor. He has written a great number of poems, mostly on American subjects and the live topics of the day, together with several prose volumes.



NATHANIEL P. WILLIS was born at Portland, in Maine, January 20th, 1807, and was educated at Yale College, New Haven. He is well known as a playwright, novelist, tale-writer, poet, and editor. He was connected with General Morris, until the death of the latter, in the publication of the *Home Journal*, and still edits that popular sheet.



GEORGE WITHER was born at Bentworth, near Alton, in Hampshire, England, on June 11th, 1588, and was educated at Magdalen College, Oxford. He studied law at Lincoln's Inn, but, like many of his contemporaries, abandoned his profession for literature. He sided with the Parliament in the Civil War, and obtained the rank of Major. Cromwell made him Major-General of Horse and Foot in the county of Surrey. After the Restoration he was committed to the Tower, on account of a seditious publication, and remained imprisoned for three years. He died on May 2d, 1667.



WILLIAM WORDSWORTH was born at Cockermouth, in Cumberland, England, on April 7th, 1770, and was educated at St. John's College,

Cambridge. He received the degree of Doctor of Laws from Oxford, in 1839; and after the death of Southey, was made Poet Laureate. He died in 1849.

WOTTON, SIR HENRY . . . . . . PAGE 45

HENRY WOTTON was born in Kent, England, March 30th, 1568, and educated at New and at Queen's College, Oxford, where he took his Master's degree in 1588. He travelled several years, and then entered the Earl of Essex's service. He was Ambassador to Venice under James the First, but finally took orders and became Provost of Eton, dying as such, during 1639.

WYAT, SIR THOMAS . . . . . . 11

SIR THOMAS WYAT, the elder, was born at Allington Castle, in Kent, and educated at Cambridge. He was a favourite with Henry the Eighth, and was celebrated for his wit and good companionship. It was said of him that he caused the Reformation by a joke, and the fall of Wolsey by a seasonable story. He lost the favour of the King at one time, probably from a too great intimacy with Anna Boleyn, but, after suffering imprisonment, regained his former position. He was sent to conduct the Ambassador of Charles the Fifth from Falmouth to London; and in his eagerness to perform the duty acceptably, over-heated himself, and caught a fever, from which he died in 1541, in the thirty-eighth year of his age. Besides his songs and sonnets, he translated parts of Virgil, and made a version of David's Psalms. The latter is not now extant.

THE END.